HER RUNAWAY DUKE

A BEAUTY AND THE BEAST RUNAWAY BRIDE REGENCY ROMANCE

NOBLE PURSUITS
BOOK ONE

ELLIE ST. CLAIR

♥ **Copyright 2024 Ellie St Clair**

All rights reserved.

This book or parts thereof may not be reproduced in any form, stored in any retrieval system, or transmitted in any form by any means—electronic, mechanical, photocopy, recording, or otherwise—without prior written permission of the publisher.

Facebook: Ellie St. Clair

Cover by AJF Designs

Do you love historical romance? Receive access to a free ebook, as well as exclusive content such as giveaways, contests, freebies and advance notice of pre-orders through my mailing list!

Sign up here!

Noble Pursuits
Her Runaway Duke
Her Daring Earl

For a full list of all of Ellie's books, please see
www.elliestclair.com/books.

CHAPTER 1

"You cannot marry him. I will not allow it."

Siena could only smile ruefully in response.

When Eliza crossed her arms and set her shoulders as though ready to do battle, it was very hard to say no to her declaration.

But the only other option was to deny her parents. Siena straightened from her slump and sent a regretful smile toward her friend, who stood a few feet away, her lips pressed together in determination.

"If only you were the one who was making the decision," Siena countered as softly as she could.

"I have no idea how your parents could expect you to marry a man so… distasteful. Unsettling. *Old*. He must be older than your father. And the way he looks at you—"

"Is how a husband is allowed to look at his wife, I would suspect," Siena said, although she couldn't help but shiver at the thought of Lord Mulberry touching her, let alone—no. She couldn't think of it, or she would never get through this day.

It wasn't his age that bothered her, although that didn't

help matters. It was how he unnerved her and the discomfort that attached itself to her the moment he walked into a room. Eliza wasn't wrong. His name alone flooded her with unease.

"I suppose the only positive of this situation is that he might not last much longer," Eliza said as she stood from her seat in the armchair before the fire and walked over to stand behind Siena, meeting her gaze in the mirror of the vanity.

Siena's lady's maid had already come and gone, having prepared her for the morning wedding ceremony, and only Eliza remained, refusing to leave Siena's side as they waited for the carriage to convey them to the church.

Siena's eyes widened. "Eliza!"

Her best friend shrugged, her blue-green eyes alighting with mischief as her dimples played in her cheeks. "It's the truth."

She reached out and stole a lily from the bouquet sitting on the vanity top in front of them and tucked it into a pin that was holding Siena's blonde hair. Eliza always described it as 'the color of sun-kissed wheat' and today it was swept up in an intricately braided style that was far more elaborate than she preferred.

But it didn't matter, for who would ever see it but her family, her groom, and his children?

"Children" who were older than she was.

"How your parents could do this to you, I will never understand," Eliza said, shaking her head with her hands on her hips now. Siena knew that Eliza meant well, but it was easy to say such things when she had parents who allowed her to do as she pleased.

"They are most concerned that I am well looked after," Siena said softly.

"You are too kind. I suppose it doesn't hurt that your new husband's family is so well respected in social circles," Eliza added in a jaded tone.

"I suppose not," Siena admitted, looking up and meeting Eliza's eyes, noting the pity in her friend's gaze.

"You do not have to do this, you know," Eliza murmured, and hope sprang in Siena's chest before she could tamp it down.

"What other choice do I have?" Siena asked, throwing her hands up in the air. "I have asked my parents for more time to find another suitor, but my father and Lord Mulberry are old friends and he refused to deny his request. This is how it has to be, whether I like it or not."

"There is always another option," Eliza said slowly. "You just might have to take a risk." She looked from one side to the other, as though someone might hear her. "If you want to escape, I will help you."

"*Escape?*" Siena stood, startled. "How? And where would I possibly go?"

"Anywhere," Eliza said, reaching out and taking Siena's hands in hers, more fervent now. "But I do have a plan. I wasn't sure if you would agree, but just in case, everything is prepared, including a horse with saddlebags packed. I do not live far, and my father won't notice a horse missing from his stable for a time."

"That would be stealing!"

"That is what you are most concerned with right now?" Eliza said with a sigh. "Honestly, Siena, do you always have do what others tell you, whether it is right or wrong? Your selflessness is to be admired, but it also drives me mad."

Siena hated the shame that washed through her at Eliza's words, especially as she knew her friend was right.

"If I do not marry Lord Mulberry," she began, as that hope began to rise in her throat once more, "then no one will ever have me. I will be ostracized and then I will never have what I truly want."

"Which is?"

"To be a mother," Siena said softly.

Eliza's eyes bore into hers. "You do understand what you have to do to become a mother, do you not? Or should I remind you? For it is very important that you know before you marry Lord Mulberry."

"Of course I know," Siena said, hiding her eye roll. "You have shared with me all of your 'knowledge' before."

"Just making sure," Eliza said. "You make it sound as though I have experience when really it is all from studying—"

She was interrupted by a knock at the door before Siena's lady's maid, Alice, opened it a crack.

"My lady, it is time for you to proceed to the church."

"Thank you, Alice," Siena said before dropping Eliza's hands. "We should go. I do thank you, Eliza. You are like a sister to me. I know you are looking out for me in the way you feel is best."

"Someone has to do it," Eliza said grimly, "for you certainly do not look out for yourself."

Eliza's words stayed with Siena as they left the house on Grosvenor Square and entered the carriage, where her mother was already waiting, her face set in disapproval.

"I do hope that you shall be more attentive to your husband's time," she said with a sniff. Siena ignored her, used to her barbed remarks, although she could sense Eliza balking behind her.

"Where is Father?" Siena asked, dropping her lilac skirts around her as she and Eliza took a seat across from her mother. She hoped Eliza wouldn't say anything to anger her mother. Eliza's parents were of proper enough standing for the daughters to be friends, but Siena's mother did not conceal her disapproval for the outspoken Eliza nor her lenient parents. Similarly, Eliza didn't hide her disdain for Siena's mother, who had always been the domineering sort.

While Siena wouldn't have to obey her for much longer, she knew she was only trading one puppet master for another.

The closer they drew to the church, the faster her heart began to pound. While she hadn't been particularly pleased about the marriage her father had arranged, she had tried to ignore it until now, knowing that there was nothing she could do to stop it so what was the point in worrying over it? She had tried in vain to appeal to her brother, but he was merely her father's mimic and was happy to marry her off so that he would never have the risk of her being dependent upon him after their father passed.

This wedding was inevitable now, and the closer they drew to St. George's, the more perspiration broke out on her brow at the reality that the next hour would change the rest of her life.

Her heart was beating so hard it was nearly pounding out of her chest, and her vision threatened to blacken completely. Her chest tightened so severely she wasn't sure she would be able to take another breath.

For so long she had set this away from her mind, pretending that it wasn't happening – but it was too late to pretend any longer.

This was real.

She was going to be married.

To Lord Mulberry.

As the panic set in, she looked to Eliza, and her friend, understanding her better than anyone, set her lips in a firm line before reaching out and squeezing Siena's hand. She lifted a brow, asking Siena what she wanted to do.

Siena only paused for a moment before she nodded just once, clenching her jaw.

She had always done what she was told, had never taken a

chance or done anything for herself. Everything she did was to make those around her happy.

But not today.

She would do it.

She would escape this wedding.

* * *

"Would you like me to light the fire, Your Grace?"

"No."

Levi sat in the worn navy damask chair in front of the empty hearth, staring into where flames should have been flickering, warming him and the room.

Which they would have were he a different man, one without his demons.

"It is rather cold—"

"Light the rooms you are using if that will keep you warm, Thornbury."

"I am not concerned for myself, Your Grace, but the staff—"

"Light the rooms for them, then. Leave this one."

"Very good, Your Grace."

The butler closed the door softly behind him, leaving Levi alone in the drawing room, dark but for the light emitted from the three large windows. On the rare sunny day, the room would be alight, but today, on a day as gloomy as his mood, it simply cast a blue glow around the room, although it was enough to read the paper before him.

He should have ended his subscription months ago, but he found that as much as he hid from the outside world, he could not help his curiosity at how it was continuing on without him.

The article was small, on the bottom right side of the third page. Most readers probably skimmed over it, no longer interested. But the fact that it remained was enough to irk him. When would they be done with him?

The door opened with a creak once more, causing Levi to throw the paper down in exasperation.

"Your Grace?" Thornbury had been with him long enough that he did not shrink away from his tempers, although Levi somewhat wished that he did.

"I told you, Thornbury, I do not want a fire."

"It is not that, Your Grace. You have a visitor."

Still facing away from the door, Levi sighed as he rubbed his fingers against his temples. "Tell Fitz to go away."

"I had a feeling you would say that," came his friend's far-too-jovial voice from behind him. "So, I showed myself in. Thank you, Thornbury. I appreciate your attempt at properly announcing me."

"Lord Fitzroy," Thornbury murmured before the door shut with a click behind him.

Levi tried to surreptitiously place the scandal sheet in the book next to him, but Fitz was too fast. Levi envied the light, unburdened skip in his step as he took a seat in the chair next to him, reaching out and snatching an untouched sandwich from the tray on the table between them.

"Still reading that shit, I see."

"It is drivel, yes, but drivel people read," Levi muttered. "Why will they not leave me be?"

"It is not every day a man survives your experience, ascends to the highest ranks, and then responds by hiding himself away in a run-down estate outside of London," Fitz said, crossing one knee over the other and then bouncing it up and down. The man could never sit still, always moving in one way or another.

"You make it sound as though I am someone to be admired."

"You are."

Levi snorted. His friend couldn't have been further from the truth.

"I came to share a thought with you."

"A letter would have sufficed."

"And miss this electrifying conversation? What a shame that would be. Besides, how would I know that you would open and read what I had to say?"

Levi remained silent, for Fitz had a point.

"You have been in hiding long enough. It has been over a year and, as you say, there is still much speculation as to what has become of you. A man becomes a duke and suddenly disappears? Many think you are dead, you know."

"Let them," he said before adding, "They also think I'm a murderer. Which I am sure is worse."

"No one is saying that much anymore. The issue is, you have done nothing to rebuild the entailed estate and you have a dukedom that could sorely use you, Levi."

"They do not need me. Others are seeing to it."

"It's not enough," Fitz said, leaning forward, his elbows on his thighs as he looked closer at Levi, but Levi refused to meet his gaze.

"What is this 'thought' of yours?" Levi asked, wanting to be done with this. He both loved and hated Fitz's visits. As much as he enjoyed seeing his oldest friend, he also hated that they always brought him a spark of hope that life could go back to the way it used to be.

That, however, was impossible.

"It has been long enough. If you return to London and society and show your face, then all the rumors will be put to rest, and no one will talk any longer. It will also be much better for you than sitting here in this awful mausoleum. Did you know it is freezing in here? And I am not talking about just the temperature, although that is also an issue. When was this place built? Surely there was another in your possession you could have chosen, although I do appreciate how close to London you are, for I enjoy the ride."

Levi stared at him, blinking as he tried to sift through all of the nonsense that had come out of Fitz's mouth.

"You think I should show my face in London? *My* face?" His mouth dropped open. "Surely you are jesting."

"I would never jest," Fitz said, pausing a moment before bursting into laughter, although Levi remained straight-faced. "Very well. I would jest. But not about this. What are you going to do, Levi, sit here alone staring at the wall for the rest of your days?"

"There are servants here."

"Besides Thornbury, Mrs. Porter, and your creepy valet, they are all terrified of you."

"They have reason to be. And McGregor is as misunderstood as I am."

"I find this place morbidly depressing."

"It fits, doesn't it?"

"You need heirs."

"No, I don't," Levi shrugged. "I do not much care about my family line, and someone will take over what is left of the mess that remains."

"Is that any way to honor your family?"

"They are not here to care," he said, pausing a moment before adding, "nor will I be when an heir becomes an issue."

His words were true, but there was more to it. To have children, he would need a wife. While he was sure that some poor woman could be forced to marry him for his title alone, he was not about to saddle anyone with the horror of staring at him for the rest of her life.

He had no choice.

He would remain here in hiding. Alone. As it should be.

CHAPTER 2

As Siena, her mother, and Eliza walked up the stairs to St. George's, the first notes from the organ wafted outside, although Siena's senses were so heightened that she couldn't concentrate on what song they were playing.

Eliza caught her gaze, giving her a nod that Siena was sure to instill confidence.

"Don't worry," she mouthed, and Siena's eyes widened as she tried not to allow her hands to shake.

Not worry. Eliza had no idea what it was like to be inside Siena's mind, for it was now a whirlwind of worry.

What if this plan didn't work? What if her mother suspected what she was going to do? What if she was caught? What if—

"It is time. Your father is waiting for you within. We have already caused a delay and we must be sure the baron doesn't have to wait for his bride any longer than he already has," her mother said. "Come along."

"I know, Mother, truly I do, but I have a slight problem," Siena said, her eyes meeting Eliza's for a moment before quickly flicking away. Eliza had whispered to her what to say in the few moments they'd had alone after her mother had first descended from the carriage, but it had seemed so much easier at that time.

"A problem?" the viscountess said. "Now is most certainly not the time for problems."

"I must…" she swallowed hard before forcing herself to say the words. "Relieve myself."

Her mother's eyes narrowed, veins in her neck straining as she leaned toward her. "You cannot be serious."

"I am," Siena said, her words breathy, but she was proud of herself for continuing. "I believe it is the nerves. I would wait, truly I would, but I cannot any longer for fear of ruining my dress."

Her mother sniffed loudly to show her displeasure.

"We do not have time to return home."

"My family's home is but steps away in Hanover Square," Eliza said helpfully. "I will accompany Siena and we will return in minutes."

Siena began to bob up and down to show how desperate her situation had become, and her mother waved a hand at her. "Stop that at once. Go. Be quick about it."

Her mother called to the footman who was still with the carriage to accompany Eliza and Siena across the street to Eliza's home. As her parents were both inside the church, there was little chance they would see anyone within but for the servants.

Eliza linked her arm with Siena's as she hurried them to the house which was, fortunately, just out of sight from St. George's.

"Come, let's go," she said as she pulled Siena around to the back of the first house as fast as their skirts and kid slippers would allow them. They reached the mews and then continued down the street to find the stables and a stablehand who was not as surprised as Siena would have expected him to be.

"Here you are," he said, leading a horse out, and Siena looked at Eliza in shock.

"Did you prepare for this?"

"I have been preparing for this for a while," she said grimly. "I had everything ready on the chance that you would actually agree to escape. We don't have much time. The horse is yours for now. I have included a map within one of the saddlebags that will lead you to Streatham. From there, you can take a stagecoach and my cousin is prepared to meet you in Crawley. She will provide you with a place to live until you decide what you would like to do next. I have written to her with the particulars, and she has promised to be discreet. I would trust her with my life. In the saddlebags is all the money I had available for you. It is not nearly as much as I wish I could have given you, but it was the best I could do. There are also a few changes of clothes."

Siena stood still, blinking her tears away. "Eliza, I… I don't know what to say."

Eliza leaned in and wrapped her arms around her in a quick embrace. "Just write to me when you are settled so that I know you are safe. I wish I could go with you or be of more help. You will likely have to work, but you would be an excellent governess. Or perhaps you can marry a man who might not be noble but could take care of you. And if you do decide to return and choose to marry the viscount, then blame it all on me."

"Oh, Eliza, there will be such scandal," Siena said as she started to consider just what it would mean to actually take this option and leave. "How are you ever going to explain my disappearance? Perhaps I shouldn't—"

"Siena," Eliza said, taking Siena's hands in hers. "Do not concern yourself for me. I have prepared your escape and I have also prepared an explanation. What do *you* want? Don't think. Just feel."

"I want to be in a happy marriage with children to love."

"You can still have all of that. But we both know there will be no happy marriage with Lord Mulberry."

"Very well," she said, trying to absorb some of Eliza's confidence in the future. "Thank you, Eliza. For everything."

"Thank me by looking after yourself," she said. "And don't forget me."

Siena stepped toward the horse, accepting the stable-hand's offer to mount it.

"Goodbye, Eliza."

"Goodbye, Siena. And Godspeed."

* * *

Siena hated the dark.

She had left London early enough that she should have reached Steatham on Eliza's map in a very short time, but she must have become lost along the way for it had been hours now and the sun was beginning to lower beneath the horizon with no sign of civilization in sight.

Which she should have known was a risk. She had never had to read a map before, so why would it suddenly become a skill she could master?

Eliza would have been able to do so, Siena thought glumly as the weight of her current circumstance, her hunger, and her exhaustion from not sleeping the night before due to her worry over her impending marriage began to overcome her. A tear of despair leaked out of her eye, which she wiped away angrily, annoyed that it had even come to this.

She was even vexed with Eliza for suggesting this – which was a rarity, for she was never upset with Eliza, especially when she knew that her closest friend in the world was only looking out for her.

It was just that, Eliza would have been able to do this, which caused her to believe that Siena was equally as competent. Siena just wished that Eliza would realize that they were not the same person, and that she was not nearly as capable.

Soon enough, the only light she would have to see by would be the stars above her and the crescent moon that had already made an appearance. She knew that anyone with experience would stop and set up camp, but what was she supposed to do? She had no way to start a fire, nothing to eat, and nothing but her cloak to sleep in. She would likely freeze. She should have just married the creepy viscount. It would have been better than freezing to death in the middle of the forest, would it not?

Then she pictured him again, remembering his lecherous gaze and comments about what to expect on their wedding night.

Maybe not.

She knew she would be best to keep moving, but her horse was growing weary. She had heard the trickle of a nearby stream for a while now and knew she had no choice but to stop. Her legs trembled beneath her as she dismounted after so long in the same position, and she had to pause for a moment and hold onto the horse until she could recapture her balance. Giving him a pat in thanks, she began to lead him toward what she thought would be the source of the sound, which must be around the copse of the trees to her right.

She had just rounded the largest one when she came to a sudden, abrupt stop.

For there, just a few yards ahead of her, was a group of three men in dark clothing, sitting in a circle, tricorn hats perched upon their heads and pistols prominently worn around their waists. They didn't notice her at first, so intent were they on items sitting on the ground before them.

Siena was already backing away, her heart in her throat, when she belatedly realized that what she had seen glinting from the ground was jewels.

These men were thieves, perhaps highwaymen.

Would they care about her and that she had seen them?

And as quietly as she thought she was walking backwards, her left foot, now clad in boots that Eliza had provided, snapped on a twig, which caused one of the men to look up swiftly.

He caught her gaze, and she scrambled up on the horse as fast as she could, pure fear fueling her actions, backing him up and then urging him to run.

But she had a feeling that she just might be too late.

She pushed her horse on, but he was tired and neither he nor Siena knew the ground nor their direction. As though sensing her hesitation, he paused, just long enough for Siena to hear a shout from behind her.

It was enough for her to regain her senses and urge the horse on, finally finding the road once more. Where it led to, she had no idea, but she could only pray that it was frequented enough that she had a chance to come across another person, one who might help her.

She hadn't made it far when she heard the hoofbeats closing in on her, and she hated the whimper that emerged from her lips. She had thought her situation dire before, but that was nothing compared to her current predicament.

The men pulled even with her before her first tear could fall, and she willed herself to hold it within, to remain strong on the outside no matter how much she was falling apart within.

This had all been a mistake. She never should have gone

against who she was. She should have done what she had always done, been the good girl and not questioned what her parents thought best for her. Look at the consequences of her disobedience.

What would Eliza do in this situation? Before Siena could come to a conclusion, however, one of the men blocked her way forward with his horse, while the others closed in behind her and she had no choice but to come to a stop.

Her entire body shook as she fought to find a way out of her predicament, dread growing when she could see no escape.

"Well, well, well," one man said, eyeing her from her feet up to the riding hat that still perched on her head, although rather vicariously at the moment, "what do we have here?"

"I am no one," she said, swallowing a sob. "Please, let me continue on my way and I will forget I ever saw you."

"That is a very fine dress you are wearing," said the next one, ignoring her words. "A lady, alone in the middle of the road at this hour?"

"I am not alone," she said, trying to keep her lip from trembling as she grasped for the words that would convince them to leave her be. "My husband is around the corner. He is a very powerful man, and I would suggest that you leave before he finds you."

One of the men started laughing. "Do you truly think we are concerned about one man?"

"You should be. He can make life very difficult for you. Go, before he arrives."

She hoped that they wouldn't realize just how desperate her tone had become as she willed them to believe her.

"We shall take our chances," said the third, the bearded one, who the others seemed to look to as their leader. "Now, pretty lady, why don't you come with us?"

The grin that spread across his face as he looked her up

and down reminded her of Lord Mulberry, and a shiver overtook her.

"I think I will be going instead."

But they had her surrounded, and when she tried to move her horse a step forward, they blocked her in further.

"We asked nicely but you actually don't have a choice," said the oldest of the three. "We could use some company tonight."

Overwhelmed by panic, she looked one way and the next, finding a newfound strength within her as she searched for any way out of this. She had run away from one lecherous man today; she would not do so only to fall into the hands of others.

Then she jumped, along with the startled horses, when a shot rang out through the air.

All of them paused for one shocked moment before two of the men began to panic, circling their horses as they searched for the source of the shot.

The third man fell off his horse, his surprised expression frozen forever on his face.

Siena opened her mouth and screamed.

CHAPTER 3

Fitz was right. Levi couldn't sit still and stare at the walls of this cold, empty estate all day, waiting for his life to pass him by.

Which was why Levi went out riding three times a day. Surging through the fields around the estate was the only time he felt like his old self. It was a heavily wooded area, and he enjoyed meandering through narrow paths while also giving his horse free reign to gallop over stretches of open areas.

Sometimes, he allowed his horse to choose their direction. It was not as though Levi had anywhere to go, anywhere to be, or anyone waiting for him, so what did it matter? Tonight, the ironically named Lucky had decided on the road more travelled, the one that led away from the estate. Perhaps Lucky had been listening to Fitz and was trying to return him to London.

"Sorry, Lucky," he muttered. "I said no to Fitz, and I will say no to you too."

Suddenly Lucky increased his pace as though he had

sensed temptation before him, and Levi peered out into the darkening sky.

"We should be heading back," he said, trying to turn the horse's head, but Lucky continued to pull forward – which was when Levi heard it too. A shout ahead of him.

Instead of allowing the horse to run ahead, he slowed him down, leading him off of the road, close to the line of trees so that they would be hidden from anyone who lay in wait.

Levi knew that he should turn around, to leave this trouble to itself and return home, but old habits were sometimes difficult to break.

He had spent enough time with a rifle in his hand that the pistol was already out and trained ahead of him.

Using his legs to push Lucky slowly forward, the four figures on horseback soon came into his view.

The three men with their distinctive tricorn hats were fairly easy to identify. Likely highwaymen who had stopped on a side road on their way to London to trade in their goods.

Levi couldn't quite make out the person in the midst of them, however. When he heard a female voice, his stomach sank as he knew they had likely come upon a woman, one who would be far too tempting for such men to dismiss.

The fact that she was alone was troubling – had they done away with whoever had been accompanying her?

"We asked nicely but you actually don't have a choice," he heard one of the men say. "We could use some company tonight."

Levi had no wish to become involved in this woman's problems. None at all. Nor did he have any desire to take on highwaymen, especially ones who were willing to use violence to get their way. But he had not become so much of a beast that he would allow who was most likely an innocent woman to be taken by these men.

He sighed as he brought the pistol up, pulled the cock fully back, trained the first man in his sights, and then pulled the trigger.

* * *

"What in the bloody hell was that? Linus?" One of the remaining men shouted as the other began to back his horse away, looking from side to side. They had both pulled their pistols, but neither seemed to know where the shot had come from. Siena took some perverse satisfaction that they were the ones now panicking.

Siena knew that she should run, but at the moment she was frozen in indecision. Was she safer to stay where she was or to turn around and try to escape? It was becoming difficult to know just which decisions were causing her more danger.

When the second gunshot sounded and the second thief clutched his knee as bright red blood spurted from it, she had to breathe deeply to keep from becoming further affected and trust the shooter could aim around her. The third man turned his horse around and bolted away, trying to outrun her surprising savior.

Siena herself looked around in shock, but no one was coming forward to try to claim her in turn.

"Who is there?" she called out, trying to instill bravery into her voice. "Are you still here?"

She waited, holding her breath as her heart hammered against her ribs, and it was another minute before she finally caught sight of the figure on horseback slowly walking toward her from the trees ahead.

"Th-thank you," she said as he neared. "You saved me."

He reached up, touching the brim of his hat, keeping his head tilted so that the wide brim concealed his face beneath.

"Had yourself in quite the predicament."

"I did," she said, a hiccupy sob escaping along with her words and she slapped a hand over her mouth to keep it in. "I thought—I thought—"

"You thought right," he said grimly. "Good thing you had Lucky."

"I am not sure I understand."

"My horse," he said, gesturing forward. "Name is Lucky."

"Oh, I see," she said, still not completely understanding. "Well, thank you, Lucky. And thank you—I am sorry, what is your name?"

"Don't need to know it," he said with a slight shake of his head. "Where are you going?"

"It is a very long story," she said with a quivering breath. "I am lost, however. Do you know how far Crawley is?"

"Day or so," he said. "Wouldn't take long to return to London, though."

"No," she said quickly. "I cannot go back there."

She waited for him to ask why, but he just sat there, still and silent, obviously not caring about her reasons.

"What happened to your companion?"

"My companion?"

"I assume you are not out here alone."

"I am, actually," she said, lifting her head, not appreciating that a stranger would feel the need to pass judgement on her actions, as right as he might be.

"Was stupid to be out here alone," he said, and her mouth fell open in shock.

"Did you just call me stupid?"

"I said stupid to be here alone," he said, his voice low and gravelly still. "What did you think was going to happen?"

"Well, I hadn't planned for this," she said, and he snorted, looking away from her. As he did, she caught a glimpse of the right side of his face, noting the beard that covered it as well as a handsome, princely profile.

"Why are you alone?" he finally asked, sighing as though he hadn't wanted to know the answer, but realizing he had needed to know.

"I ran away from my wedding," she said, and his head lifted as though he was going to look at her, but before the brim of his hat rose completely, he lowered it once more. She had to admit that she had liked what she had been able to see, from the prominent cheekbone, down the strong jawline to plush lips on the one side of his face.

"My parents were forcing me to marry a man who was over twice my age, you see," she said. "Which was not so much the issue, but the fact that he was rather the lecherous type. There were stories and – well. My friend convinced me to escape, but now I think I would have been best to stay and take my chances. It would have been better than highwaymen."

She took a breath, realizing that she had likely said far too much.

"Thank you for saving me," she said, more quietly now. "Where is the closest place that I could go for shelter for the night?"

He didn't say anything, just sitting there, and a chill began to creep down Siena's spine. Somehow, she had this innate feeling that she could trust this man, but he was so quiet. Perhaps he had only gotten rid of the highwaymen so that he could have her for himself.

"Thank you again, sir," she said. "I-I shall go now. I did not mean to cause you trouble."

She turned her horse to walk away, but she hadn't travelled more than a step or two when his voice called out.

"Stop."

She paused, her horse following his command.

"You can come with me."

"Thank you but I shall continue on," she said. "I would not mean to cause you any more trouble than I already have—"

"I have an estate nearby. When we arrive, my housekeeper will see to your needs."

"Your housekeeper?" she repeated, intrigued that he would have an estate. He must be someone with means, although his intentions might not be any better than those of the highwaymen. But he had saved her. "Who are you? And where are we?"

"Near enough to Chiswick," he said. "Who I am does not matter."

He turned his horse – Lucky, he had called him – back toward the way he had come, leaving her with the choice to follow or remain behind.

She looked behind her into the night, and then at the retreating back of the insufferably rude man in front of her. He had called her stupid, and yet he had saved her life. What was she to do?

She closed her eyes and let her heart's intuition speak for her.

And took a chance.

* * *

Levi shouldn't care whether the girl followed him or not.

She was just a slip of a thing, and clearly frightened by him.

And she hadn't even fully seen him.

The last thing he wanted was to take her back to his estate, but he couldn't very well leave her in the middle of the road with night falling. He was worried about her and had a strange sense that it was up to him to protect her.

Her story was far-fetched, and yet the gown peeking out

from beneath her cloak was quite fine. Pieces of fair hair were falling out over her shoulders, but aside from her dishevelment, her delicate features and thin, fine jewellery were those of a well-bred woman.

He would give her a place to stay for the night and then return her to London and this despicable fiancé tomorrow. It was all he could do.

"I know you think me a fool," she said softly behind him, apparently having decided that he was the less threatening option compared to the dark woods. "It seemed the best decision at the time, and I had a plan. It just… went awry."

He said nothing, allowing her to keep talking. Her voice was sweet and melodic, flowing over him in waves, somehow soothing his tortured spirit.

"Where did you learn to shoot like that?" she asked.

"The army."

"You were in the army?"

"I was," he said with some hesitation, unsure if she would think that was a positive or negative. Not that it mattered.

"You are not anymore, then? Were you injured?"

"You are inquisitive."

He supposed after the day she'd had, she deserved to know more about the man she was following.

But all she needed to know was that he was best to be avoided.

* * *

Siena studied the back of the man in front of her. He was tall, with broad shoulders and a build that tapered closer to his hips, although it was difficult to tell with his cloak billowing behind him. As darkness had fallen, he had lifted his head, no longer hiding his face beneath the brim of his wide, unfashionable hat.

Siena couldn't help but be intrigued by this shadowy figure, as much as she should likely be fearful. His silence, compared to most people in her life, was something of a refreshing change, even if his grunts were frustrating.

She had more questions, but after the surge of unwelcome excitement, fatigue was beginning to set in through her entire body, and she had to fight to keep her eyes open. They must have closed for a moment for suddenly her entire body was jolting upright, her heart pounding once more as she realized she had nearly fallen off of her horse. Her companion never looked back, never turned around to see if she was still following him let alone still attached to the horse. He probably didn't much care and was only now doing what was expected of him.

Siena was about to ask how much farther they had to go when a building rose up in front of them, seemingly from nowhere. The first thing she noticed was the portico, supported by columns with triangular pediments crowning on top. Beneath was a grand entrance, to the sides symmetrical wings fanning out with identical large, rectangular windows that had an odd look of eyes peering out into the night.

It must just be the light, she considered, wondering if the grey hue of the building was also from the darkness or if it was truly as dreary as it appeared.

Second-floor balconies adorned with wrought-iron railings stuck out of the sides like leering grins and Siena shivered at the sight of the cold, austere building.

She looked around, expecting to be led up an ornate drive trimmed in hedgerows similar to the estates she more currently frequented, but instead, the landscape around them was nearly barren, borders of garden blocks the only signs of memories of previous opulence.

"Do you live here?"

Her voice came out as more of a squeak.

"I do," he said, swinging down from his horse with ease before taking the reins of hers, lifting a hand to help her down.

Her legs were numb from being so long on the horse and when she swayed right into him, he caught her, an arm coming hard and strong around her.

"Steady," he murmured in her ear as though he were speaking to a horse.

Siena barely noted the groom appear and take their horses, likely round to a stable, as her exhaustion threatened to overwhelm all.

The man led Siena up the front stairs beneath the massive portico, not offering his arm but staying a step behind her as she held onto the railing. The moment they stepped through the front doors, he called out, "Mrs. Porter?" as Siena surveyed the entrance, the dome on top of them covered in stained glass that she could imagine cast beautiful colours around the entryway in the daylight.

Soon enough, a plump woman clad in black with a surprised expression on her face that quickly fell into a welcoming smile appeared in the front entrance.

"Who do we have here?" she said, looking from Siena to the mysterious man, who appeared to be the master of the house, and back again.

"I found this young woman being accosted by highwaymen," he said, his voice back to its curt gruffness. "She has had a trying day and needs a place to stay. Just for the night. Help her, Mrs. Porter?"

"Of course," the woman, Mrs. Porter said, coming to Siena and taking her hands in hers. Siena felt reassured and safe with the woman, and suddenly she wanted nothing more than to curl up and sleep, protected by this strange house and people she had never met before yet seemed more trustworthy than those in her own family.

She turned around to thank the man, but her attempt was in vain.

He was gone.

CHAPTER 4

"Your Grace?"

"Yes, Thornbury?" Levi said, looking up from the book he was attempting to read in the armchair of his bedroom, set next to the bed instead of by the hearth. A fire was simmering across the room, covered by an extra grate overtop, necessary for warmth at this time of night in his first-floor bedroom.

"I hear we have a visitor."

The butler had such effusive cheer in his voice that Levi had to sigh.

"She is only here overnight, Thornbury, until she can be on her way in the morning. I encountered her while on my ride. She was in trouble with nowhere else to go."

"I see," Thornbury said, although clearly, he did not see at all, for he was practically beaming. "She appears to be a beautiful young woman."

"I hadn't noticed. Nor does it matter."

"Mrs. Porter has her settled in the pink bedroom."

Each bedroom of the house was accented in a different colour, although most had faded at this point with the light that shone in the long windows and the balconies along with lack of upkeep. This estate had not been frequently used until last year, and Levi didn't plan on having any visitors to keep it up for.

"Very good," Levi murmured, keeping his head down in his book before he realized that the butler's arrival, while irritating at first, might serve a purpose. "Thornbury, in the morning, can you and Mrs. Porter please see that the woman has a proper meal and then have one of the footmen escort her to Crawley."

"We are happy to do so," Thornbury said, but then paused, not leaving the room as Levi wished him to. Finally, Levi had no choice but to raise his head to look at him.

"Is there more?"

"It is only a suggestion, but knowing how you love to ride and that the woman appears to be comfortable with you, perhaps you might like to—"

"No."

"My apologies, Your Grace, I was only—"

"I said no, Thornbury. Are you the duke, or am I?"

"You are, Your Grace, of course."

"Goodnight, Thornbury."

"Goodnight, Your Grace."

Any regret Levi felt at how he had spoken to his butler fled as he considered the thought of the woman seeing him in the daylight. The less comfortable she felt here, the better. Then she would be on her way and never have any reason to see him again. If there had been any other option, she would not be here at all, but all he could do now was make sure she departed as quickly as she had arrived.

He placed his book down as he allowed his mind to wander over the events of the evening. He had no regret in shooting those men. He assumed the first was dead and the second would be in time unless he was seen to by a proficient physician, which was doubtful. They were not the first men he had killed, and they were certainly not innocent in their actions. Had he come upon them simply stealing goods he would have left them be, but he could never have ignored the woman with them to be debased.

The woman. She had provided him a good deal of information about her predicament, but she had never mentioned her name nor who she was. Likely from a family as noble as his own.

Not that it mattered.

Nothing did.

Not anymore.

* * *

As tired as she was, Siena hadn't been able to prevent herself from staring as the housekeeper led her to her bedchamber. She wasn't sure how she couldn't. This manor was unlike any she had ever seen before – and she had seen quite a few.

Paintings covered nearly every surface, of family members and landscapes and inanimate objects. If she had the opportunity, she would spend more time tomorrow enjoying them, for it was like being in a museum, albeit an empty one, devoid of any visitors.

"There does not appear to be much staff," she remarked to Mrs. Porter, who took small but quick footsteps.

"We have only the master to look after," she said, tucking a few grey curls back into their pins. "Most of us have been here for years and it was always just a few of us until he arrived. It has been nice to have someone to look after."

"The family didn't live here before?" Siena asked, interested in learning more as the housekeeper showed her into a bedroom. It had an air of disuse, but that was to be expected with no preparations.

"The maid will be here in a moment to ready the room for you," Mrs. Porter said with a smile, although she quite clearly had avoided Siena's question on purpose.

"I never realized there was such a large manor so close to London," Siena said. "I am surprised I have not heard of it."

The housekeeper began humming a tune as she pulled down the bedcovers.

"Have you any belongings with you?" she asked.

"Oh, yes, a few in my saddlebag. I completely forgot about them," Siena said.

"No matter. The footman has likely seen to it."

There was a knock at the door and the housekeeper bustled toward it, opening it to a maid who held a bundle in her arms.

"Here we are," she said, placing it on the bed and opening it up, finding a nightgown within. Her new belongings were as much of a surprise to Siena as to the housekeeper, for Eliza had packed it.

"Let us get you settled. Then in the morning, we will make sure you go to where you need to be. Everything is better in the light of day."

Siena nodded, wondering if she would see the master of the house again.

"Might I ask... whose estate is this?"

The housekeeper paused, turning to look at her with a serious expression on her face, which appeared to prefer jovial matters. "You do not know?"

"No. Your employer is not exactly... forthcoming."

"I shouldn't be the one to tell you, then."

The housekeeper placed Siena's clothing down on the bed, looking over her shoulder at the maid, who was lighting a fire, before returning to Siena and taking her hands in hers.

"If there is anything you must know about the master, it is that he is all bluster. Deep within, he has a kind heart, even if he doesn't realize it himself. He has had a rough go of it recently."

"I see," Siena said quietly, allowing the maid to help her undress. She wanted to ask more but sensed that it wouldn't get her anywhere.

"That is a beautiful gown," the housekeeper said in an apparent attempt to restore their good humor.

"Thank you," she replied softly. "I was supposed to be married in it."

"Were you now?" That captured Mrs. Porter's attention.

"I have a favour to ask," Siena said in a rush. "It seems to me that this is a house of some secrecy, judging by your master's inability to provide me with his name. Can I ask you to also keep a secret for me – the very fact that I am here? There are… circumstances that I have no wish to return to."

"Of course," Mrs. Porter said with that cheerful smile again. "We can keep a secret, can we not, Mary?"

"We most certainly can," Mary said, standing when all seemed to be well.

"Good night, dear," Mrs. Porter said as the two of them began backing out of the room. "We shall see you in the morning."

And with that, she shut the door on Siena, along with any of her questions.

They would have to wait until later. For her exhaustion gave her no other option but to fall asleep.

* * *

Siena woke the next morning with a strange feeling that something was amiss, but she couldn't quite put her finger on it.

Then she opened her eyes to the faded soft pink canopy floating around her head, and it all came rushing back. The wedding. Her escape. The highwaymen. Her rescue.

Now here she was, in a strange manor so close to London and yet so far at the same time.

Yet, somehow, despite the cold draftiness of her surroundings, she was comfortable here. Perhaps it was the knowledge that nothing was expected of her, that no one cared who she was or what she was to do with her life.

Perhaps it was the way the lord of the manor had saved her without expectation of anything in return and how the servants had welcomed her.

Whatever it was, she felt a good deal better about her decision now than she had when she had been lost in the woods, prepared to freeze to death.

A large crack rent the air, startling Siena, and after recovering from how high she jumped, she pulled the covers up to her chin in pretense of some kind of protection. It was then that she noticed the incessant splattering upon the window, and she slid her legs out of bed, pulling her wrapper tightly around herself as she walked toward the balcony, peeking out of the casement doors to see that a thunderstorm had gathered through the night. The dark clouds loomed ominously, casting a gloomy pall over the formerly serene countryside. Rain cascaded from the heavens, pounding against the windowpane with a rhythmic intensity that made Siena's heart quicken.

Mesmerized by the raw power of nature, she turned the latch of the casement doors and stepped outside, her bare feet slippery on the stone of the balcony. The overhang above her prevented her from becoming soaked, although the wind still pushed droplets of rain against her skin and whipped her hair backwards. The air was thick with the scent of wet earth and the distant rumble of thunder rolled through her ears, sending shivers down her spine.

In the midst of the storm, flashes of lightning illuminated the sky and the rolling hills beyond the manor grounds. The lush green meadows and vibrant wildflowers seemed to dance under the duet of light and sound.

Siena's eyes traced the path of a lone droplet as it meandered down her windowpane, its journey mirroring her own. No longer was it carefully controlled, held in balance, but instead was making its own path in whatever way it wished to turn.

Her thoughts turned back to her predicament. She glanced over at the wardrobe to find her fine lilac gown hanging in front of it. It appeared to have been washed and pressed already, although she had no idea how anyone would have had time to do so unless they hadn't slept.

As she opened the wardrobe to find what else awaited her, a knock sounded on the door and Mary, the maid who had attended to her last night, awaited.

"Oh, my lady, the balcony!" she said, rushing across the room to close the doors.

"That would be my fault, Mary," she said regretfully, noting the water that had splashed across the floor. "I couldn't help myself from wanting to experience some of the storm."

"It is a powerful one, 'tis," Mary said, turning and joining Siena at the wardrobe to help her dress for the day. "I suppose you will not be leaving this morning, then."

"No, I do not suppose I will be," Siena murmured as she lifted her arms for Mary to help her don her chemise and then lace her stays. "Is there breakfast prepared?"

"There is. The cook is happy to have another mouth to feed, my lady."

"Wonderful. Thank you, Mary."

Siena was filled with optimism as Mary led her to the breakfast room, hopeful to have the chance to properly thank her host. After sleeping well, she was feeling much better and ready to face the day and whatever came with it. A day without expectations, actually, which suited her quite well.

Only, her host never showed his face at breakfast.

"How are we this morning?" the housekeeper said, entering the room with a smile.

"Quite well, thank you," Siena said. "I am not sure if I properly introduced myself, but I am Lady Siena."

"It is wonderful to have you with us, Lady Siena," Mrs. Porter said, turning to leave, but Siena called out to stop her.

"Will the lord of the manor be joining me this morning?"

"Likely not, my lady," Mrs. Porter said with a not-unkind smile. "He does not enjoy visitors."

"I see," Siena said quietly, even though she didn't understand whatsoever, for he was the one who had brought her to his estate. "Hopefully I will have the chance to see him later today. He did me a great service and now has allowed me to stay in his home. I hope I am not too much of an inconvenience, for I doubt I will be able to leave today as planned."

"No, the roads will be impassable for a few days, I am afraid," Mrs. Porter said. "But we will do whatever is necessary to keep you comfortable here."

"Thank you, Mrs. Porter."

Siena took a small sip of her tea, her mind already working on a plan to show her gratitude towards this mysterious man.

She was undoubtedly curious about him, but more importantly, she owed him her life. Before she left his company, she would find a way to repay him for his kindness.

It was the least she could do.

CHAPTER 5

"What do you mean, she is still here?" Levi asked Thornbury through gritted teeth. "I told you that I wanted her gone by morning."

"Your Grace," Thornbury said as he stood in the door of his bedchamber, holding his hands out in supplication as he pointed to the curtains covering the windows. "Have you looked outside yet today?"

"No."

Thornbury crossed the room and drew back the curtains a few inches. "A significant storm has arrived. There is no way for the carriages to traverse the mud outside."

Levi let out a growl that he knew was quite unduke-like, but it was only Thornbury to hear.

"Keep her to the main areas of the house – the front parlor, if you can. I will be in my study this morning and will take my tea there. Arrange for her to leave as soon as the paths are clear."

"I will, Your Grace, but it could be a few days until the roads dry after the storm lets up. Perhaps you should greet her properly. It might be nice to have some company."

Levi fixed him with a look that he hoped would portray his thoughts on the subject and dash any of Thornbury's hopes.

Thornbury threw his hands up in the air as though giving up before walking out the door, only to be replaced by Levi's valet. Thornbury was more outspoken than most butlers, but of course, he also knew that it was quite unlikely Levi would relieve him of his duties since Levi had no wish to hire someone he knew might run the moment they arrived.

Thornbury had known him since he was a child, so he had ensured that the staff looked after him and his house no matter how much Levi scared them.

When Levi was finally ready for the day, he used the servants' staircase to descend the stairs and find his way to his study, annoyed that he had to sneak around his own property. This was why he never arranged for anyone to be in the house.

He wished he could escape for a ride, but of course, this morning the ground was far too wet and the rain falling far too hard for it to be a safe one, for him or his horse.

Levi couldn't help but wonder how the girl fared today. Thornbury had been right – she *was* beautiful, not that it mattered any. He wouldn't be looking upon her again.

When he reached his study, he didn't take a seat behind the desk but instead walked over to the group of chairs around a small table in the corner, turning a chair around so that he could see out the window, watching the dance of light across the sky as the rumbles still sounded, some so strong that he could feel the vibrations through his chair.

He didn't have long to wait before the footman arrived with his breakfast, and Levi sat back, kicking his feet up against the windowsill as he ate a piece of toast with his tea.

He was so mesmerized by the lightning that split the sky that he didn't hear the door open.

It was her scent that gave her away first. That light smell of peaches that had followed him home last night.

He stiffened. Had no one told her not to enter?

"Leave me be," he said, keeping his feet planted where they were.

"My lord – I assume you are a lord?" she said, her voice soft and light, making him almost feel guilty about how harshly he was speaking to her – almost.

"Something like that."

"I do not mean to pry. I am simply uncertain what to call you."

That made some sense.

"Call me Levi," he said, hoping she would go now.

"Very well, Levi," she said to his back. "I am told that you had wished me to leave today, but unfortunately the weather conditions make that impossible."

"I see that."

"However, I believe it might be fortuitous, for I would hardly like to leave without the opportunity to properly thank you for what you did for me."

"No need."

He could sense her hesitation at his abruptness, but he had to respect her for continuing on, regardless.

"I told you that I was going to Crawley, but the truth is, I do not even know the person I am to meet there. She is a friend of my friend's, and I am not even certain that I can afford passage to reach her now that I took the complete wrong direction. I was thinking, perhaps I could stay here and work for you. First, to pay back my debt and then perhaps I could earn some money from you."

Her words had come in a rush, as though she was uncertain of what she was saying and now they hung in the air, waiting for his response.

He took a breath.

"Lady Siena, is it?"

"Yes," she said, surprise in her voice. "How did you know that?"

"My servants tell me things," he said.

"You might as well call me Siena, if I am to refer to you familiarly as well."

"Very well, *Siena*," he said, the twist in his words necessary for he wanted her to lose any feeling of comfort she had about staying here. "There is no debt to be paid. There is no work for you to do. All I want is for you to go when you are able. I do not want you on my estate. I do not want *anyone* here. Do you understand?"

He heard her sharp intake of breath, and for a moment felt a slight bit of guilt, but this was necessary.

"I—" she began sharply, but then in a lower voice continued, "I do not understand why you wish to be alone."

"It is not for you to understand," he said bitterly. "Just go. In fact, I will give you the money to go, if that is what it takes. My footman and driver will see you wherever you choose to journey to, if needed."

She was silent for a few moments before finally responding.

"Very well," she said so quietly that he almost didn't hear her. "I will go as soon as I am able, I promise, but I am told that the roads will be impassable for a few days at least. I do apologize for being a burden, but until I leave, perhaps we could be friendly?"

For a woman who seemed so timid, she certainly would not take no for an answer. Levi sighed, realizing he had run out of options. There was only one sure way to deter her.

He kicked his legs back down from the windowsill before pushing himself up to stand.

And then, he slowly turned around.

* * *

Siena was on the verge of tears. What had she done so wrong that this man was so desperate to be rid of her? He had made it clear that he thought her a fool, to which she agreed with him, but now that the situation was finished, why could he not at least attempt to be friendly with her since they were stuck here together?

She was twisting her hands together, trying to determine just how to apologize, when he finally stood from his chair. He turned around slowly, the right side of his face coming into view first. Lit only by the blue light entering through the window behind him, she was once again struck by how handsome he was, despite the sharpness of his features. Then he turned all the way to face her, and she had to bite down on her bottom lip to prevent her gasp from escaping.

For as handsome as the right side of his face was, the left side was nearly destroyed. Scars lined his cheek, a patch covered his eye, and the corner of his lip was twisted. The raised skin continued down his neck to beneath his jacket, and she imagined that the scars continued down his body – and perhaps internally as well.

She had been trying to understand him. Now it was finally making sense.

The right side of his face twisted to match the left.

"Not so interested in staying now, are you?"

His voice was taunting, angry, but there was more beneath it – pain. Worry, likely that she would do the very thing he was asking her to do and run away.

Instead, she took a few small steps toward him so that she could better see him.

"That looks painful," she said softly.

"You have no idea," he bit out.

"No, I do not," she agreed. "And yet, I can understand your reluctance to allow people close to you."

His forehead furrowed. "Does it not disgust you?"

"No, why would it?" she said, lifting her shoulders. "I am sorry for whatever happened to you, that is for certain, but I must say that I am much more put off by the way that you speak to me than your scars."

He snorted then in what she could describe as near to a laugh. "You must be joking."

"I am not." She paused as pieces of the puzzle began to click into place in her head. "You are the Duke of Dunmore."

"Took you long enough to figure it out."

The bite remained in his words, but Siena was well aware why. He must know of what the scandal sheets said of him, the rumors that circled about him. She wasn't one to pay them much attention, but everyone within the *ton* knew about the scandal that was the Duke of Dunmore.

"I am sorry for the loss of your brother," she said quietly. "That must have been quite difficult."

"You do not know the half of it," he practically sneered. "But suffice it to say that if Reginald was here instead of me, you would be much better off – you and everyone else."

"How long has it been?"

"Just over a year."

"So, you are still in mourning, then."

He turned his head, studying her. "Are you not frightened?"

"Why would I be?"

"Some say I murdered my brother. You are fine with being alone in a room – in an estate – with a murderer?"

The pain was so evident that it was heartbreaking, and she shook her head.

"From what I can tell, you would give anything to have your brother back and not be sitting here in this current predicament. Besides, if you were the kind of man who would hurt me, you would not have helped me escape from those ruffians and then invited me into your home and left me untouched."

"Perhaps that is why I want you to leave. So that you do not tempt me."

She laughed wryly. "I doubt that is the case."

He said nothing to that but studied her with the one blue eye that she could see.

"Well," she said, not knowing where else to take this conversation. She had questions, of course, as this man had been the subject of much speculation and here he was now in front of her, the duke who had disappeared. But he was clearly not inclined to share, and to push would likely have him letting her out into the rain. "Do you have a library?"

He seemed startled by her change in discussion, but he nodded. "Of course."

"I shall go peruse it, then. If you wish to spend any time together, I am more than happy to do so. Good day, Your Grace."

She strode toward the door and had just opened it when he made a grunt behind her, and she looked back over her shoulder.

"Levi," he said, already turning around to return to his seat but she could still hear him. "Just call me Levi."

CHAPTER 6

Why the hell did she have to be so… sweet?

Levi had been sure that revealing his scarred face would have sent her running back to London and her lecherous fiancé, but instead, she had been kind. Understanding. She had even offered her condolences for the loss of his brother.

Then she had taken herself off to the library as though nothing had changed. It was perplexing, that was for certain.

Everyone else had a rather intense reaction from their first look at his face. Some hid their grimaces, others couldn't help but allow them to show.

But she had just continued to look at him as she always had.

Levi hardly knew what to do with himself around her now. For so long he had hidden away in his estate to avoid the pity and fright of others.

Lady Siena certainly hadn't been scared. He could tell that his experience had upset her, but it wasn't pity that he had seen on her face. It was understanding.

It was the way he had wanted people to react, but the first

time anyone had ever accepted him for who he was and not who he had been or for what had happened to him.

He had been so rude to her that his attitude was likely what would have her running away once the rain cleared.

Unbelievable.

Unable to sit still in his study any longer, he began a slow walk down the corridor. As much as he told himself to go elsewhere, his feet had other ideas as they walked him toward the library, where Lady Siena awaited. His boots tread slowly over the carpeted floor before pausing in the doorway of the library, which had always been his favorite place in the entirety of the estate, the jewel in the otherwise dull stone of the building.

She was standing in the center of the room, her feet planted firmly on the plush carpet's circular design. With her head thrown back and her arms gracefully extended, she twirled slowly in circles, taking in the countless books that surrounded her. Levi had no claim in the design of this magnificent library, but he was determined to keep it just as it was. Reading was his only other source of joy besides riding - a way to escape from his reality for a brief moment.

He had barely scratched the surface of the vast collection before him, but he wanted to savor every section so that he would never run out of options. As he gazed at the woman now walking before the shelves, delicately running her fingers over the spines, Levi couldn't help but watch in admiration. Even though he should have entered the room and announced himself, he found he was enraptured by her presence. She radiated a peaceful energy that filled the space around her.

She stopped when she reached the writing desk, taking a seat behind it and lifting the quill pen. She ran her fingers over the feathered edges before dipping it in the inkwell and touching it to the paper. She tucked her head and began to write, her hand moving in broad strokes.

Levi wondered what she was writing, and whether the writing was for herself or others.

He couldn't have said how long he watched her – minutes, certainly, but he had nowhere else to be – before she stopped, sat up, folded the letter together, and then dipped the seal in wax and stamped it.

She stood, and before she could turn to the door and catch him watching her, Levi slipped backward into the drawing room, stopping in an alcove as she marched by him to the dining room.

"Thornbury!" he heard her call out cheerfully. "I have a letter. When the rain clears, could you please have it posted for me?"

"Of course, Lady Siena," he said, and when Levi heard her shoes pad softly down the hallway, he stepped out and followed the butler.

"Thornbury," he called out when he was sure Lady Siena was out of earshot.

"Yes, Your Grace?" Thornbury said, turning around with a larger smile on his face than he had ever seen before.

"May I have that letter?"

"Which letter?" the butler asked.

"The one that the lady just gave you."

Thornbury appeared confused but held it aloft.

"She has asked me to post it."

"I shall do it."

"You shall… post it?"

"Yes," he said. "I will take care of it."

Thornbury was clearly unsure of that idea, but it wasn't for him to decide.

"Of course, Your Grace," he said, passing the letter over,

which Levi tucked into his jacket pocket before entering his study – alone.

He could feel the butler's eyes on him as he continued within and shut the door behind him but paid him no mind as he took a seat behind the desk and broke the seal of the envelope.

He didn't want to break her confidence, but he also couldn't risk that she would tell anyone about where to find him or what he looked like.

When he opened the letter and began reading, he couldn't help his sigh of frustration.

For that was exactly what she had done.

> Dear Eliza,
>
> I must thank you again for the risk you took in helping me to escape. It must have been greatly difficult for you to return and explain my absence. I hope you did not find yourself in any trouble on my account.
>
> I promised to write when I was settled, and I am - somewhat. However, I did not make it to your friend's residence.
>
> Unfortunately, I do not possess the sense of direction that you do, and I found myself lost along the way.
>
> Fortunately, I was welcomed to an estate near London. You will be shocked to learn of my whereabouts. I am at the home of none other than The Duke of Dunmore. Do not be concerned, for he is not nearly as frightening as all would

have us believe, despite the injuries he has obviously sustained. You know how rumors are.

I am told that the estate is not far from Chiswick. Perhaps one day you can arrange to come and visit me, or we can meet there to catch up with one another.

He lives alone, but his servants are most kind and gracious. I am going to take my time to determine my next steps as I do not wish to be a burden upon your friend, and this household has proven they are adept at keeping secrets.

Sending you all of my love,
Siena

Levi took one last look at the letter, crumpled it into a ball, and then threw it in the fireplace.

* * *

SIENA WONDERED when a woman had last lived in this estate.

There were books, yes, but besides that, there wasn't overly much for her to pass the time doing. No needlework, no watercolours, no one to take tea with.

So, she read and she wrote poetry, for which she was rather inspired by the landscapes outside of the windows, as dreary as they were.

But she became bored of even that over the day, and eventually, she decided to go exploring.

She wondered if she would see the duke. Ever since their confrontation in the study that morning, he had made himself scarce. She guessed that he was still hiding in the room, where he was least likely to come upon her.

As she entered the drawing room, however, she saw that the door to the adjoining study was open, and she peeked inside, finding it empty. She knew she should leave and not invade his private space, but she couldn't help wondering what he kept himself busy with inside.

Siena stepped cautiously into the study. Tall bookshelves lined the walls, filled to the brim with leather-bound volumes, their spines worn with age. The scent of old parchment and ink hung in the air, reminding her of the magnificent library she had discovered this morning, where she intended to return once she completed her perusal of this estate.

Her eyes were immediately drawn to the imposing oak desk that dominated the center of the room. It was meticulously organized, each item in its designated place. Quills stood perfectly upright in an inkwell, while stacks of paper lay neatly arranged on one corner of the desk. A golden pocket watch rested beside an ornate letter opener, its intricate design catching Siena's eye.

Curiosity got the better of her as she approached the shelves, her fingers trailing lovingly over the spines of countless books. Each volume seemed to hold a secret waiting to be unraveled. Siena's heart quickened with anticipation as she carefully pulled out a weathered leather-bound book.

The cover opened with a low crack, the pages inside revealing delicate illustrations of exotic plants, their vivid colors dancing across the pages, transporting her to far-off lands she could only dream of.

Lost in the magic of the study, Siena hardly noticed the rain drumming relentlessly against the windowpane. The dim light from outside cast long shadows across the room, giving it an air of mystery and intrigue.

As her eyes continued to wander, Siena's attention was drawn to a beautiful landscape hanging on the wall behind the desk, contrary to any study she had seen before, which always held a portrait in a place of prominence. It made her realize how devoid the house was of any personality.

She began to shiver, but it wasn't from the empty estate. It was the cold. There was a chill in the room that had settled into her bones as she looked through the book, and she realized then what was missing – there was no fire in the grate. Instead, the fireplace remained empty, waiting to be filled. Did he ever light a fire in here? She wondered as she wandered over for closer inspection, finding that the few ashes were long cold.

Her eyes caught on paper that was lying on the bottom of the grate. It was the same stationary she had written upon just this morning, she realized as she reached out a hand and plucked it out. In fact, that was her handwriting upon the page.

Her brow furrowed as her eyes ran over the letter she had written to Eliza, fury growing inside of her. How did the duke think he had any right to not only read her letter but set it aside to be destroyed? Before she could decide just what she was going to do about it, the door creaked behind her, and she whirled around to find the duke's imposing figure filling the frame.

"What do you think you are doing?" he ground out, and she jumped, startled.

"I was simply wandering the estate," she said, telling herself to stand her ground, that she was not in the wrong here. "As I did so, you must understand how surprised I was to find a letter that I wrote to my friend in your fireplace, prepared to be burned!"

He started, and she realized then that perhaps her choice of words had disconcerted him.

"You do not seem to understand the meaning of secrets," he said, passing beside her, his body just brushing against hers as he took a seat behind the desk, crossing his arms over his chest as he stared her down. She appreciated that he was no longer hiding his face from her, as annoyed as she was with his actions. No one should feel ashamed for having been injured. It was his words and actions that upset her.

"Eliza is my closest friend in the entire world, and she would never tell another where I am or who I am with," Siena said, willing herself to be patient. "She was the one who helped me escape."

"A fine job she did of it," he muttered, and Siena, most annoyed that he would insult Eliza, walked over to the desk, flattening her palms down upon it.

"You could have asked me to rewrite it," she said. "What if I had never found it? I would not have known that Eliza did not know where I was or who I was with."

"All the better."

"You… you…" She tried to find the words. "You are not very nice."

He scoffed. "I've been called worse."

"I will be writing her again," Siena said resolutely, crossing her arms over her chest.

"Do show me what you've written next time."

"It is personal correspondence."

"Not when it is being written from my home."

She took deep breaths, rubbing her temples as she began to pace back and forth in front of him.

"How long until the roads are passable again?"

He looked out the window and shrugged. "First the rain would have to let up. After that, I would say we have a few days, depending on how much sun we get. In a hurry?"

"I thought you wanted me gone."

"I do."

"Then I will leave as soon as I am able. You clearly do not want me here and I am not particularly enjoying myself with you. I do not like to be an unwelcome house guest and you have not allowed me to do any work for you to repay you."

He sat forward, looking up at her. "Fine."

"Fine, what?"

"Fine, I have work that you can do."

He said nothing else, and she waited, until finally, she asked, "Are you going to share anything else about it?"

"You can inventory the paintings."

"Inventory?"

"Go through this house and make a list of the paintings," he said, waving his hand around. "No one has lived here for years, and I have no idea if any of them have value or if they are the work of some ancestor who fancied themselves an artist."

"How will I know the difference?"

"Write down a description. A name if you can see one. Then I can send the list to an art connoisseur."

Siena actually liked the idea. It would not only give her purpose but also a reason to inspect all of the paintings that decorated the house in closer detail.

"I would be happy to do so."

"You seem to know where to find writing paper," he said wryly, and she nodded.

"That I do."

She stood and began walking to the door but stopped, turning around. "Will I see you at dinner?"

"No."

"Why not?"

He stared straight ahead, which kept the left side of his face away from her. It was a head tilt that he did often, and she wondered if he was hiding that half of himself on purpose or if he was doing so without noticing.

"I prefer to dine alone."

"Is my company really so bad?"

"No," he said. "Mine is."

"It does not have to be that way."

"Trust me. It does."

He bent his head and opened a book in front of him, effectively dismissing her.

So finally, without another word, Siena did as he wished.

She left.

CHAPTER 7

Levi stayed true to his word and avoided Lady Siena for the next day, taking his meals in his bedroom so that he wouldn't have to see her.

The truth was, he rather liked conversing with her. Thornbury was right. She was beautiful, but more than that, she seemed to respect and enjoy the company of everyone she encountered. She spoke to the staff as though they were members of the *ton* and didn't seem to treat him any differently despite having seen the fullness of his face and cheek.

He caught glimpses of her diligently working on her list, and he appreciated her efforts. He had no idea if he would actually be able to afford to pay her or not, but he would make certain that she could get to wherever it was she wished to go.

As for him, he would be staying right here. He had travelled enough of the continent, although not for reasons he preferred to consider at the moment. He was leaving those memories behind him, shutting them out of his mind along with the life that had been before.

Feeling cooped up in the house, he decided that he would

attempt a ride. Lucky didn't mind a light rain, and it seemed that it had diminished enough that they could at least stay to the manicured paths, although they were rather few and far between.

He donned his riding garments, hat, and cloak, and raced through the rain toward the stables, surprising the stablehand when he entered through the door.

The scent of fresh hay mingled with the earthy musk of horses, creating what was, to Levi, an intoxicating aroma.

A row of gleaming saddles lined one wall, each one meticulously cared for and lovingly oiled. Bridles hung from hooks, their supple leather glinting in the soft light, and a thick layer of straw covered the floor.

In one corner stood his massive black stallion, his mane flowing like liquid midnight and his eyes burning with an untamed fire. His muscles rippled beneath his sleek black coat as he pawed at the ground, knowing that Levi's arrival meant it was finally time to leave the stable.

"Your Grace," the stablehand said as Lucky gave a whinny of welcome. "I tried to tell Lucky there had been too much rain, but he doesn't seem to care."

"Nor do I," Levi returned, walking over and patting the horse's sleek neck, taking solace in him when he butted his head up against his shoulder. "We won't be long. I think we both need to run. The rain is not as heavy as it was."

"Very well."

It seemed to take far too long until Levi was out in the field, giving Lucky free rein. The horse took his offering and stretched his legs out, sleekly galloping over the wide expanse of land.

It gave Levi the chance to consider his houseguest, and just what he was going to do with her.

He couldn't very well turn her out, but she had said that she had a place to go. He had promised that one of the servants would see her there, but he wasn't sure if he trusted any of them enough to accompany her.

He couldn't very well do it himself. If they were discovered, he'd have to marry the girl, and then he would never be alone again.

And solitude was what he wanted.

Or was it?

* * *

SIENA WAS HEADING up to the long gallery to begin on the most voluminous collection of paintings in the house when a flash outside the window caught her eye. She walked over to the small keyhole window, stood on her toes, and looked out over the soaked green fields before her.

She wondered if the duke had ever ventured into the hills in the distance.

She would ask him when he returned.

If he returned. Or even wanted to speak to her.

She was well aware that he had been avoiding her. The thought made her shrink a little inside. Was she truly that terrible to be around?

She had always been the girl whose company everyone enjoyed. The amiable one. The dutiful daughter. The lady who could make pleasant conversation without drawing much attention to herself.

None of that seemed to matter to the duke.

The duke who everyone talked about.

He was hiding something – that much was obvious.

The scandal sheets were rife with speculation as to what had happened to his parents, his brother, his family's entailed estate.

Siena didn't read the scandal sheets, but her mother did, and she was forever commenting on the latest gossip.

In this case, she said there were tales of everything from the duke murdering his brother in cold blood and then setting their estate on fire to hide the evidence, to the duke going mad in battle and then returning home and hiding from society due to the shame of what he had done.

The only parts of it that Siena knew were true were that the duke had no other remaining immediate family and he had fought Napoleon until his brother died when he was home visiting. She wasn't sure that anyone truly knew the rest of the story.

Siena was not a woman who based so much of her decisions on fact and rational thinking. She just knew, deep within her, that the duke was not a man who would ever hurt someone close to him.

Even if he had killed one of the highwaymen without any inkling of remorse – at least that she could see. She supposed that was a result of his time in battle.

The motion outside returned, and she was startled to see a streak of black across the expanse of land before her. There might not be much in the way of cultivated gardens on this estate, but the natural landscape was breathtaking.

As was the speed of the horse. Lucky. He suited the duke, the two moving together in grace and fluidity. Perhaps Lucky wasn't so inaptly named. If it hadn't been for him, she would never have been discovered by the duke. She shuddered to think what would have become of her.

The Duke of Dunmore was a mysterious man, that was for certain.

Whether she would ever solve him was another story.

* * *

LEVI COULD ADMIT that his spirits were much improved when he returned to the house after his ride. Lucky had also been appreciative, snorting with a shake of his head as they returned to the stables, as though thanking Levi for ignoring the rain.

Levi entered the house with some trepidation, on the lookout for Lady Siena. He didn't know what he had been expecting of her, but he had thought she would be far more… passive, perhaps remaining in her room as she waited for the skies to clear and the roads to dry.

He didn't like how she, instead, wandered the estate as though she was a house guest at a country party.

He asked his valet, McGregor, to draw him a bath, sitting and resting his sore leg while the footmen prepared it.

It wasn't until everyone had departed except for his valet that he started removing his rain-soaked clothing.

"This might hurt," McGregor said as Levi lifted his arm and McGregor began to slowly peel the wet fabric off of it. Levi flinched as it tugged at the scar on his shoulder but didn't voice any of his pain. It was nothing compared to what the pain had been a few months ago.

He was healing slowly – on the outside at least, although he would never be the same again.

McGregor finished helping him undress and held an arm out to assist Levi into the bathtub.

He hated relying on someone else, but his leg was stiff from the cold rain, and he had no desire to injure himself any further.

He sighed as he sank into the bathtub, the warm water welcoming as it washed around him, soothing his sore muscles.

"Ye push yerself awful hard, Your Grace," his Scottish valet said. They had served together in the war, and he was one of the few people that Levi trusted. McGregor had no family to speak of before joining the war effort and when it was time to leave, Levi had offered him a position at his estate.

When Levi had been injured, McGregor had remained, despite his responsibilities becoming so vastly altered from what he had agreed to. McGregor treated him differently than he had before – with more reservation, perhaps concern at how Levi might react to him – but he had remained loyal.

"I know, McGregor," he said. "But it feels better than not."

The valet nodded his head and passed Levi a book before departing, shutting the door behind him. Levi relaxed into the bathtub, holding the book in front of him to read while he soaked. He couldn't simply sit and bathe without it, for then his mind could wander, which was a most terrifying prospect.

He was making his way through Shakespeare's works and was currently on King Lear. It was tragic, yes, but he far preferred focusing on fictional tragedies than his own.

Levi stayed within until the water grew cold. McGregor was not far, in the small room adjoining his own, but now that Levi's muscles had warmed, he would be fine to step out of the bathtub himself. He stood, the water sloshing over his torso, and reached for the towel next to him.

He had just lifted it to dry his face when he heard the turn of the doorknob, and he lowered it, prepared to tell McGregor that he didn't need his help.

Only, it wasn't McGregor who stood in the doorway.

It was Lady Siena, eyes wide, mouth open in shock.

* * *

SIENA HAD BEEN EXPLORING the second story in this east wing of the house. Most of the rooms were empty of nothing but old furniture that still bore dust and cobwebs, the rooms clearly unused.

She now understood why her room was described as "the pink room," for every bedroom was decorated in an entirely different colour, like a house composed of pieces of the rainbow.

She should likely return to the long gallery and finish her inventory of the art pieces there, but it was far more interesting to walk from room to room. Each bedroom held one or two pieces, and these seemed more intimate, as though they were created for various members of a family.

Who had lived here and what would they think of the estate's current resident?

Siena was lost in thought when she opened the last door of the second-story hallway, which was in the same wing as her bedroom but at the opposite end of the corridor.

She should have taken her time, to determine whether anyone was within.

But when she opened the door and saw the duke, she hadn't been able to look away.

She should have apologized.

She should have shut the door.

She should have run down the hall and away from the room.

Instead, she stayed still, her eyes drawn to his body.

He stood in the bathtub, water dripping off defined muscles.

Siena's heart raced as she watched the duke dry his face, completely unaware of her presence. The grey light streaming through the room's large windows illuminated every detail of his tall, lean form.

His strong shoulders glistened with droplets of water, causing her breath to catch in her throat as she drank in the sight before her, mesmerized by the sheer raw masculinity exuding from this man.

A surge of desire unlike anything she had ever experienced before washed over her, her cheeks flushing with a mixture of embarrassment and excitement.

She couldn't help but take in the scar that didn't stop at his face. Instead, it ran down his entire left side, from his neck, over his shoulder, down his left torso and left leg. It was red, raw, and puckered, and she winced at how much pain he likely felt from it. Was it the scar of a past battle? If she had to guess, it appeared to be a burn, one he would likely never fully recover from.

His towel covered the bottom of his face and draped over the middle of his body. Siena felt rather wanton for wishing that she could see more of him, as her eyes couldn't stop returning to where his manhood was hiding.

The duke finished drying his face, lowering the towel and lifting his chin.

When he caught sight of her, he froze, his one good eye locked upon her. For once, he wasn't wearing the patch over his left eye, which was sealed shut, the skin around it cracked and red.

She gasped at how painful it must be, and that was when his face twisted until he was wearing the same nasty scowl he had when he had first shown his entire face to her.

"What are you doing?" he growled at her as he wrapped the towel around his body, hiding himself.

"I-I was exploring the bedrooms, l-looking for art," she said, stammering at the anger that emanated from him.

"In my bedroom?" he said, the volume of his voice rising.

"I didn't know this was your bedroom," she said, her arms flailing wildly as she tried to explain. "If I had any idea, I would never have entered."

"Wouldn't want to see this monstrosity, would you?" he sneered, and she stepped back as though he had slapped her, such was his ire.

"It's not that," she said. "I j-just wouldn't want—"

"Get out," he said, his voice calm, low, even, and she took a step back, nodding, although her feet wouldn't seem to move of their own accord.

"I said get out!" he shouted now, and she jumped, tears welling in her eyes as she quickly backed out of the room, slamming the door behind her as she ran down the corridor as though she was being chased.

She made it all the way to her own bedroom, where she threw her writing materials down on the bed before collapsing in the middle of it and allowing the sobs to emerge.

CHAPTER 8

How had her life come to this? To being shouted at by a reclusive duke for only doing what she thought would help him?

Siena wasn't sure how long she remained prostrate on her bed feeling sorry for herself before a slight knock sounded on the door. She wanted to tell the person to go away, to leave her alone, but, of course, not wanting to hurt any feelings as the duke had hers, she sniffed, wiped her eyes, and called out a watery, "come in."

Mary stood in the door, a hesitant smile on her face.

"I heard the shouting, my lady. Are you all right?"

"I am fine, Mary, thank you," Siena said, dipping her head, pulling at the embroidery that covered the pink bedspread. "I am afraid that I am not very welcome here, is all. I am trying to be helpful, but I seem to only become more of a burden."

"'Tis not your fault, my lady," Mary said, taking a step into the room and shutting the door behind her. She took a seat on the bench in front of the vanity, close enough that they could speak in lowered voices but not so close that she was in Siena's space. "The duke has had a trying time of it, and I am afraid that any who become close to him often face his wrath. It has naught to do with you."

Siena nodded. "It is not just that. It is also that I simply am not welcome anywhere. I cannot return home. The duke does not want me here. I do have a house to go to, but until the roads are passable, I will not be able to get there. I cannot even send a letter to my friend. I would say I am a prisoner here, except that my jailor has more interest in setting me free than I do myself."

She laughed wryly at that, and Mary tilted her head as she studied her.

"Well, know this, my lady. You have a friend in each of us here. I know it seems the duke can be hurtful, but the truth is, it is good to see him with others in his presence. It has been a year since his brother's death, and he has had nearly no visitors in that time, save for one determined friend."

"It seems I have only left one beast to find another."

Mary lifted her hand to try to hide her gasp. "That is how the duke describes himself. Has he said the word to you?"

"A beast?" Siena furrowed her brow. "I only called him such because of the way he has treated me."

"I wouldn't repeat it around him. He will think you mean his scars."

"His scars are the least concerning of all of him!" Siena said, shocked. "Is that why he has hidden himself away?"

"Wouldn't you?" Mary asked, and Siena had to pause, considering it. The question, however, was such a different one, for as a woman, she lacked most choice that was associated with such a decision.

"I am not certain what I would do," she admitted. "But if I had the option, I would prefer to continue to be close to those I love."

Mary rose from her place. "I must return to my work, but know that you are not alone, my lady."

"Thank you, Mary," Siena said quietly. "I needed a friend."

At home, her mother had never allowed her to speak to servants in such a manner – they were for assisting, not for visiting – but it had always bothered Siena that she spent so much time in their presence to never have a conversation.

Perhaps there could be another way to live. A different way.

As for the duke... she would love to stay and show him that he didn't have to live in the pain that appeared to consume him.

But perhaps he was past saving.

* * *

Levi knew he had been a beast to the girl.

When he'd seen the way she had looked at his scar, however, every reason why he had become the man he was, why he hid away in this estate, why he never saw anyone in polite society, reared up within him. He hadn't been able to quell the emotion that emerged.

He was remorseful, yes, but he was also thankful.

For he had begun to like having her around, and now he remembered why he had to be alone.

She was a beautiful, innocent young woman in the prime of her life, who should find a man worthy of her. Hell, even her formerly intended fiancé sounded like a better bet.

Levi could never share his life with another. Not anymore. For he now only carried around the worst parts of himself. Every good part had been burned away.

He could barely hang onto his temper, and when her eyes had landed on his scar, tracing it from his sightless eye down his body, he had seen the revolt on her face. Now she would never be able to look at him without remembering the full extent of his ravaged body.

He had to be rid of her. He looked out the window now, at the drizzle that continued to fall from the sky.

"Why can you not stop raining?" he yelled at the heavens, as though they could answer him or dry up upon his rage.

But no, the rain just kept falling, mocking him, showing him that he had no more control over this than he did any other area of his life.

That being said, he knew he had to apologize. Lady Siena hadn't deserved his wrath. She had been in the wrong place at the wrong time and was likely more traumatized over what she had seen than anything else.

There was only one solution.

He had to apologize.

He sighed as he called for McGregor.

It seemed that tonight, he would be joining Lady Siena for dinner.

* * *

SIENA ENTERED the dining room that evening with a book in hand, for she expected to be eating alone and four courses took an awfully long time with no one but herself for company. She had found a collection of Shakespeare in the forefront of the library, and she had picked up *A Midsummer Night's Dream*. She far preferred Shakespeare's comedies to the awful tragedies that her mother had insisted she read.

She stopped short in the doorway when she saw the duke sitting at the head of the table. Upon her entry, he stood, nodded his head stiffly, and pulled out a chair for her.

Siena knew she was gaping and could practically hear her mother in her head telling her to close her mouth, but she couldn't help herself. Where was the man from a few hours earlier, who had shouted at her to get out of the room, who had looked at her as though she was the devil himself?

"I will join you for dinner," he said stiffly. "If you do not mind."

"O-of course not," she said, finally taking steps into the room, setting her book down on one of the side tables as she did. "It is your home."

"If I make you uncomfortable—"

"It is fine," she said, forcing a smile on her face, unable to help her need to put him at ease as he was so clearly worried about her reaction. "I would be most pleased to have company."

She had been placed to the right of him, and she wondered if that was his own doing or if the servants had set them like this, but it was no matter.

She cleared her throat to begin polite conversation, but he lifted a hand.

"Before we begin, I must apologize," he said. "The way I spoke to you this afternoon was not acceptable and I am sorry for it."

Siena found the intensity of his blue eye too much to bear and she looked down at her hands, which were currently twisted in her pale blue gown. Well, Eliza's pale blue gown that was one of the few she had packed for her.

"Thank you," she murmured. "I also apologize for entering and seeing you... unclothed." She had to choke out the word as heat rushed into her cheeks once more at the reminder of seeing him completely bare before her.

"I realize how shocking it must have been," he said, his voice rough, uneven.

"You are correct," she said, finally meeting his gaze despite how it caused the flush to rush from her cheeks throughout the rest of her body. His frown deepened at her words, pain slicing over his face. "I have never seen a man's body before," she whispered, biting her lip as she did, noting the surprise on his face.

"*That* is what shocked you?" he said, losing the awkwardness.

"Yes," she said with a frown. "Of course it did. Why else do you think I was so startled?"

He was silent for a moment before he finally answered her. "My body is… significantly scarred," he said. "I could understand how seeing its ugliness would have affected you."

Her brow furrowed. "It saddens me to think how much pain you must have felt," she said. "If anything, I was surprised at how well you move considering what it must feel like to do so."

He grunted as the soup course was brought in, his gaze down upon the bowl, frowning at it as though it had done him some disservice.

"Is something the matter?" Siena asked, leaning forward.

"I do not usually eat in company," he muttered.

"Pretend I am not here."

"That's not it."

"Then what is the problem?"

He lifted his hands to the table, and it was only then that she realized she had never seen him without gloves before – save for the incident earlier today, but with all of his manliness before her, she hadn't been paying much attention to his hands.

Now she saw that his left hand was not unscathed.

"Can you move it?" she asked, gesturing toward it.

"I can move it some," he said. "The scar tissue restricts the movement, however. It is the same with my jaw."

"Do what you need to enjoy your meal," she said. "I will pass no judgment."

"I eat slowly."

"I have all the time in the world."

They were both silent for a time, the only sound the clinking of their soup spoons against their bowls, and Siena found that there was truly nothing unpleasant about eating with him, besides her slight concern that his anger might flare up again.

He did eat slowly, carefully, but it rather relaxed her.

"Thank you for allowing me to stay," she said quietly, striving for a way to convince him to talk. "I can hardly imagine being in London married to Lord Mulberry right now."

He had just taken a sip of his wine and choked, nearly spitting out the liquid.

"Lord Mulberry?" he said, his fingers tightening on his wine glass. "*That* is who you were going to marry?"

"Yes," she said. "Do you know him?"

"I know *of* him," he said, his entire body shivering in obvious disgust. "My God, but it is fortunate you escaped him."

"Because he is so much older than me?"

The duke began to shake his head. "Because he is cruel. But who am I to talk."

"I do not see you as a cruel man," she said, a smile tugging at her lips. "A little surly, perhaps."

"Surly," he grunted, his lips turning upward into what Siena couldn't call a smile but just was, perhaps, not a frown. "What kind of parents do you have that they would marry you off to Mulberry?"

Siena bit her lip. She had thought the same and yet she instinctively couldn't help but defend them.

"They were doing what they thought was best."

He looked at her with a piercing gaze.

"You must not go back to him."

She swallowed, wanting to ask him to expand, but she was too scared of how he might respond.

"Did you sustain your injuries in the war?" she asked, not

knowing where the question came from, but she had been wondering and also wanted to change the subject.

His head snapped up at her words. "How did you know I was in the war?"

She shrugged, looking down at her plate. "Everyone knows."

"I suppose," he said, bristling. "You must know all about me, then."

"Actually, not much at all," she responded, straightening her spine. "The fact that there are so many rumours about you tell me that there is no validity to any of them. For if the truth were known, then no one would have to speculate."

He looked at her in some disbelief. "You truly believe that?"

"I do."

He paused as the footmen removed the soup dishes, replacing them with the first course, cold cuts of roast beef and pickled vegetables.

"I did not sustain my injuries in battle," he said, and Siena waited for him to continue. "I have no wish to speak of them any further."

"Very well," she said, disappointed, not because she needed to know so badly but that he didn't trust her. "Should you ever like to, I am a good listener."

He nodded but didn't continue.

Siena sensed that he had never spoken to anyone about whatever demons haunted him, and she wondered about this friend who insisted upon visiting whether the duke wanted him or not.

She hoped for the duke's sake that he would find a way forward.

She just didn't know if she would be anywhere near to see it.

CHAPTER 9

"Will ye be taking breakfast downstairs, Yer Grace?" McGregor asked with a smirk the next morning.

"No," Levi said, wincing as he swung his legs out of bed. "Why would I take breakfast downstairs?"

"I heard yer dinner last night was a success. Thought maybe ye'd be joining the lady again this morning."

"No," Levi repeated, more tersely this time. "I will take breakfast in my bedroom as I always do. Then I will dress for riding and will take Lucky out."

"Still a slight rain."

"Of course there is," he muttered under his breath as McGregor brought his tea next to the bed. "How do you know so much about my dinner, anyway? We didn't discuss it last night."

McGregor had asked him about it as he helped him ready for bed, but Levi had told him it was fine and left it at that.

"From the footmen," McGregor said.

"The footmen are gossiping about me now?"

McGregor stopped laying out Levi's clothes to look at

him. "Everyone does. Not just here, but in every household. Not much else to talk about, now is there? Never mind the chatter, Yer Grace. We only talk amongst the staff. Everyone is most loyal to ye. Not a word will get out."

He paused before beginning to speak again. "She's a bonny one, ain't she?"

Levi grunted, although he couldn't help the quiet twinge that struck deep within him at the thought of McGregor – or any of his other staff – considering Lady Siena in that way.

"Hadn't noticed," he said. "Be respectful."

"Of course!" McGregor said. "We were only thinking of you."

"Of me?" Levi repeated. "What do I have to do with it?"

"Well," McGregor said with a shrug as he helped him into his clothing for the day, "when ye've shut yerself up here all alone there is not much chance to meet women. However, it seems that one has quite literally fallen onto your doorstep! Perhaps it's fate."

"Perhaps it is nothing more than what it appears to be," Levi said, stamping down any hope of seeing Lady Siena as more than just a woman passing through – for that was all she was. And he would be wise to remember it.

The truth was, McGregor was right. He *had* enjoyed himself at dinner last night. He knew he was not a scintillating conversationalist, but Lady Siena hadn't seemed to care. She had been comfortable in the silence, and when she did speak, she was worth listening to.

He had been surprised at how quickly she had forgiven him, but then, she appeared the forgiving sort, considering what she'd had to say about her parents.

If he was the man he had been before, he would have had a mind to tell them exactly what he thought of their plan to marry her off to a man like Mulberry. What could they possibly have been thinking? He knew Mulberry had fortunes, yes, but it had been amassed from preying off men when they were at their lowest points.

While Levi wasn't certain what the man would be like with his wife, if how he treated other men – and women, or so he was told – was any hint, Siena had escaped just in time.

He wondered what she was doing today. What she was wearing. What mood she was in.

Was he so bored that this was all he had to consider now?

Except he thought he actually cared.

Which was most concerning of all.

* * *

SIENA WAS PLEASED to find the library that morning empty of anyone except for the characters that filled the pages of books surrounding her. She had been itching to discover which books were nestled in the shelves that lined the expansive room from floor to ceiling but had been too absorbed in her work of itemizing the paintings of the house.

She had saved the library for last and was pleased to find that in here, there were no paintings to speak of. Instead, the books and their spines provided all of the art one might need.

Siena smiled like a child who had been presented with her choice of sweets as she wondered just how many volumes were housed here. She crossed over to the shelf where she had found Shakespeare's works and then began to make her way to the left.

They were rather well organized, so different from her father's library, which was filled with books but only to display his collection of knowledge. He hardly ever read any of them and Siena found them far too boring.

The majority of the books in his collection were political and historical volumes.

Her preferences leaned towards distant lands, thrilling swordfights, and disguised princes.

None of which fit in her father's library.

Here, however, she held out hope, for she had no idea who the past owners of this grand room were and what they might have been interested in.

She peeked over at the next shelf, thrilled when she opened the cover of the first book and found it to be a work of fiction.

This was promising.

Over the next hour, she became familiar with how the library was organized and her eyes widened in amazement as she discovered the variety of genres present in the collection. From thrilling adventures to heartbreaking romances, the shelves held a treasure trove of stories waiting to be explored.

Her fingers trailed along the spines, finding the rough texture of leather-bound classics and the smooth surface of newer novels. Siena's heart raced with excitement as she unearthed hidden gems, each book whispering promises of wonder.

She found herself drawn to a corner of the room where a dusty old tome sat abandoned six shelves above her. She wasn't sure what it was about that particular book that sat at the end of the high shelf, but she needed to read what was in it.

Far out of her reach, she found the ladder that was attached by wheels to the shelves and rolled it over to where she required it.

Siena took a deep breath, shaking off her fear of heights.

"You can do this, Siena," she told herself. "Face your fears."

She had run away from a wedding and her family.

She could climb a ladder.

With trembling hands, she began to climb, one rung at a

time, until she reached the top and was parallel with the shelf. With one hand clutching the ladder tightly, she stretched the other out and up and carefully pulled the book down, blowing away the layer of dust that obscured its title.

"*Love for All Times*," Siena read aloud, her voice barely above a whisper. She should climb down the ladder and find a place in the library to begin the story, but she was too intrigued to wait. A quick look wouldn't hurt.

She flipped open the cover and read just a few lines, which was more than enough to capture her attention as she was immediately transported into a world of magic and mystery. The words on the pages seemed to dance before her eyes, painting vivid images of lush greenery and colorful blooms.

She was so caught up that she nearly forgot where she was, and when a voice called out behind her, she whirled around with a yelp of surprise.

And lost her grip on the ladder.

Her arms fluttered around in the air, desperately trying to catch hold of the rungs, but it was no use – her momentum was taking her backward, and there was nothing she could do but prepare for the fall.

She closed her eyes, balled her body, and landed with an "oof" in strong, solid arms.

She opened her eyes slowly, wondering how she could have been saved – and found the duke's face staring down at her.

"What were you doing?" he bit out, and she inhaled swiftly, appreciative that he had caught her and yet annoyed that he would chastise her when he had been the one to cause her to fall.

"I was finding a book."

"You were reading a book. On a ladder."

"Just for a moment," she defended herself, frowning at

him. "It had called to me, and I wanted to see what it was about. I never considered that you might appear and scare me as you did."

"Scare you? By walking into my own library?"

"Yes," she said, even though she knew he had every right to be here and had only startled her by accident. It was just that she didn't like the way he was blaming her for doing nothing untoward. "You should have announced yourself."

"I did," he said wryly, staring down at her. She met his gaze, noting that his expression was no longer angry. In fact, it was... curious. She shifted slightly in his arms, suddenly incredibly aware that they were around her body, holding her tightly as though she weighed nothing.

Siena felt a rush of warmth as she realized that despite their casual conversation, her body was pressed against the duke's. His solid arms held her securely against him, their faces now mere inches apart. His breath brushed against her cheek, his intense gaze locking with hers.

"I... I didn't mean to startle you," he said softly, his voice low and smooth, so different from the gruffness that usually filled it. "But what kind of book could be so captivating that it would lure you to read it while standing high upon a ladder?"

She swallowed hard as a jolt of awareness shot through her at his nearness. "It's a book... a love story," she managed to reply, her voice barely above a whisper. "It's handwritten and hand-drawn, which leads me to believe it might be true?"

His eyebrow raised, his gaze flickering with interest. "Handwritten, you say? That does sound intriguing."

As he spoke, Siena couldn't help but notice the way his lips moved, the slight stubble along his jawline, the scent that surrounded him, a masculine mixture of sandalwood, new fallen rain, and a sweet scent she couldn't quite identify. Her heartbeat quickened as she became acutely aware of their closeness.

Siena's cheeks flushed as heat radiated off the duke's body, warming hers, his gaze holding her eyes in a mesmerizing lock. She couldn't tear her eyes away from his, the strange pull toward him both exciting and terrifying her.

Feeling emboldened by the moment and the book still clutched in her hand, Siena took a deep breath and spoke softly, "Would you like to... read it with me?"

The words slipped out before she could anticipate it herself, but she didn't regret it. She longed for company, but not any company – his. There was more to this man than what he showed her and the rest of the world. She could feel it and thought that maybe he had forgotten it himself and needed a reminder.

She didn't know what had happened to him to make him so distrustful of the world around him, but perhaps it was just that his story wasn't finished yet.

The duke's eyes softened at her offer, his grip around her loosening slightly as he finally set her down on her feet.

"You don't want me to get in your way."

"You would not be in my way at all." Her cheeks warmed slightly as she realized how much she wanted him to agree to this. "I would appreciate your company."

He paused, looking away from her for a moment before he returned his gaze to her and cleared his throat.

"Very well," he replied softly, the faintest upturn of his lips making Siena's heart flutter.

He waved his hand toward two chairs by the window, a small table between them. She took one, noting that he winced slightly while taking the other.

"Did you hurt yourself?" she asked as now with space between them she recalled how quickly he must have moved across the room to catch her. "How were you able to reach me so fast?"

"Old habits," he said, staring out the window and off into the distance, and Siena had the distinct feeling that, for a moment, he was not with her but somewhere – or sometime – else entirely. "There was a time when I needed to be able to move gracefully and quietly to stay alive."

Her breath caught in her throat at the thought of it.

"You have lived an adventurous life."

His head swivelled back toward her, pain upon his face. "You could call it that."

She wanted to ask more, but he picked up the book she had set on the table between them.

"I have been through this library so many times and yet, I have never seen this book before."

"I cannot say what it was about it that drew my attention," she said with a shrug. "Its cover is old, dusty, and grey. Yet within it seems to hold magic."

"Very well," he said. "Why do we not begin?"

CHAPTER 10

Lady Siena thought that the book was magic, but it wasn't the book.
It was her.
He had asked her to begin reading aloud and suggested they take turns, but before he knew it, he was resting his head on the cushion of the chair behind him, her soothing voice lulling away the pain as he relaxed into the story.

As much as he had been trying to fight it, Levi couldn't help but be drawn to her. It was not just due to the beauty that was obvious in her delicate features and fair hair, but for the strength and determination that shone from her brown eyes.

As Lady Siena continued to read, the words seemed to come alive in the room, weaving a spell as they swirled around them in a dance of emotions and untold stories.

Levi found himself lost in her presence, the world around them fading into insignificance. He stole glances at her delicate profile, the way her lashes fluttered with each sentence, the slight furrow of concentration between her brows.

He found himself captivated by every nuance of her being

- the way her lips curved in a gentle smile at the humorous parts of the story, the way her eyes sparkled with mischief when she imitated different characters.

"The descriptions in this book," she commented, her tone changing at her words, "reminds me of Greystone."

"How so?" he said, his eyes closed now. "It speaks of a house full of love, light, laughter. That is nothing like Greystone."

"But the brightly colored bedooms, all in different hues? That cannot be a coincidence. I think that sometimes it is the people that make the home, do you not?"

He snorted. That said a lot about him.

"The emotion of the people, I should say, and how they feel about the house," she continued as though reading his mind, "it's all in here. How much the two people loved one another, and their hopes for a life together. Do you know anything about who owned Greystone before your family did?"

Levi shook his head. "Not much. Somehow it came to our family through a marriage dowry although when or how, I am not sure. I don't believe it has been lived in for years, however."

"If this book is true, then this was a happy home at one point in time, years ago," Siena said, her voice warm and light. "Perhaps it could be again."

Without realizing it, he had reached out to touch her. Her hand was soft and warm beneath his, but when his hand involuntarily began to wrap around hers, the tight pull of the skin reminded him of his injury. Of what he was.

He jerked his hand away, his eyes flying open as he sat upright in the chair, shocked at how he had forgotten himself.

"I am so sorry," he said as he realized she had quit reading.

"For what?" she asked.

"For touching you. With my hand. I—"

"It's fine," she said, a smile playing across her lips, the book still splayed in her lap, open to the page she had been reading. "It was a touching moment in the story and… I enjoyed a moment with you. Truly."

He stared at her, trying to determine if she was having him on, but her expression was sincere enough that he knew she meant what she said.

Levi wasn't sure what to do with her, a woman who apparently saw past the horror that covered his face. He had shut himself off from the world because he couldn't handle the looks of disgust or pity that followed him around, especially when those expressions only matched what he felt himself when he looked in the mirror or fell asleep and the memories came rushing back in nightmares.

"You enjoy reading, then, do you?"

"I do," she said, a smile stretching across her face. "Very much. I so love the idea of adventure, but since I cannot go anywhere myself, why not experience it from wherever I am?"

She was so earnest and excited when she spoke that he couldn't help but want to share in it with her, in whatever way possible.

"Anything you find in this library that you enjoy can be yours," he said softly.

"What do you mean?" she asked, her cheeks flushing and her breath quickening.

"I mean that my gift to you is any book you would like – *The Enchanted Garden*, or any of Shakespeare's works that you are currently reading or anything else that you might find."

"I couldn't," she said, shaking her head. "They are yours."

"I only like to read each book once, and I have thousands in here that I am sure I will never get through."

"You like to read as well?" she asked, her brows raising as the smile crossed her cheeks.

"I do," he said, keeping tight control over his emotions. "The stories keep me company and replace my memories."

"Are they really so bad?" she asked, leaning in, her hand coming to rest on his leg.

"They really are," he said. "War is not something to talk about in polite company."

Of course, there was far more haunting him than war, but that alone certainly hadn't been the glorious experience many ladies would imagine.

"I don't mind," she said softly.

"You would if you knew what it was truly like. Men you spoke to moments ago suddenly—" He snapped back abruptly as her question brought him back to reality, a reality in which he had no right to be sitting so intimately with a woman as beautiful and vibrant as her, especially darkening her spirit by speaking of such things.

As he stood, light washed over him, and a quick glance out the window revealed that the sun was beginning to appear from behind the clouds.

"The rain has stopped," he stated, the fact filling him with both dread and relief. "We just have to wait for the roads to dry and then you can be away from here."

And with that, he bolted from the room as though he was being chased.

* * *

WHAT HAD JUST HAPPENED?

One moment they were sitting together, enjoying a story and even bonding over their love of fiction, and the next he was running away as though she had insulted him.

Siena thought back over their interaction, not remembering anything that could have caused such a reaction in him. She sighed as she looked out over the grounds stretching behind the window, now illuminated by the sun that had broken through the clouds.

He was right. The rain had stopped. She walked to the window, crossing her arms over the book and holding it against her chest.

Was it a sign? Should she leave and discover what she was to do with the rest of her life?

Was she only comfortable here because she felt that she could hide away from the world and what it wanted from her? Or should she believe in this feeling of destiny that had brought her here – despite the duke who seemed to want her gone from his home and his land as fast as possible?

It was a question she pondered throughout the day, as she finished *The Enchanted Garden*, as she drank tea alone in the drawing room, and as she wandered the abandoned gardens outside of the library terrace doors.

The overgrown grass and tangled vines brushed against her dress as she walked through them, a reminder of the neglect and time that had passed since anyone tended to the gardens. The ground was soft and squishy beneath her boots, evidence of the heavy rain over the past few days and the lack of maintenance for the past few years.

Through the air, thick with the earthy scent of moss and decaying plants, she could hear the distant call of birds, and then, the whinny of a horse.

Lucky. She turned toward the sound, nearly expecting to see him coming up behind her once more, but all she saw was the flick of his heels and the swish of his black tail as he disappeared into the thicket of trees across the fields.

She was sure the duke hadn't seen her, or else he would have stopped and asked her in that gruff, surly way of his just what she was doing out here and why she wasn't inside within his home's protective walls.

It was interesting how the same overprotective man was the one who couldn't wait to send her away so that he could retreat into the shell of his estate once more.

Siena couldn't help herself from following the path Lucky had galloped, over the once-manicured paths and past the flowerbeds which were now littered with weeds. She picked her way carefully around the cracked and crumbling stone walls, circling the abandoned fountain as a hint of long-forgotten perfume lingered in the air, the remnants of a time when the gardens were loved and cared for.

She didn't know what she was hoping for as she followed in the path the man and horse had tread. She had no expectations of overtaking them, due to their speed, but she supposed she thought there might be something of interest in the path they had travelled.

By the time she reached the tree line, water from the rain-soaked long grass had invaded her boots but she forged on, warmed by the bright sun overhead, which beat down upon her cloak until she reached the canopy of the branches of leaves overhead.

It was both louder and quieter here on the forest floor. There was no wind nor distant noise, but the chattering of animals and insects went on all around her, calling to one another as they described all that was before them.

A murmuring caught her ear, and while she was gripped for a moment in fear at the memory of the last time she had come upon men in the forest, she was soon soothed when she recognized the voice.

She stepped out, about to announce herself, but stopped when she saw what the duke was doing. He was crouched down on the ground, but not the same unmanicured ground that surrounded him. There was a square of dirt that appeared to have been recently cultivated, and Siena gasped when she saw the flowers blooming within it.

The duke began to turn at the sound, and she jumped behind a tree to hide, but she was too late.

"Who is there?" he asked, standing with a swirl of his cloak and his hand on his hip as though ready to draw a weapon, like a warrior ready to face his foe. Lucky gave a whinny in her direction, and Siena jumped out with her hands in front of her.

"It is only me."

"Lady Siena? What are you doing out here?"

There was the gruff question she had been waiting for.

"I was walking," she said, not seeing why she would have to explain herself any further. "What is this?"

She began to round what appeared to be a garden, even as he shuffled back and forth, clearly uncomfortable.

"It is…" he struggled for words.

"It is a flower garden," she said, crouching, reaching a hand out to touch a soft, velvety petal. "The roses are beautiful."

She leaned in closer, drawn by the scent, but when she reached out to tug a rose toward her, this time she pricked her finger.

"Ouch," she said, bringing it up to her mouth and sucking on it gently.

Still not hearing any reply, she turned around to make sure that the duke was still there.

"Are you—"

She stopped when she noted the expression on his face. His good eye was fixated intensely on her finger which was still sitting between her lips. His pupil dilated, becoming darker and larger as he took slow steps toward her.

"Your Grace?" she asked, her own breath becoming

quicker and slightly erratic as his musky scent mixed with the roses around her. That was the scent she hadn't been able to identify. Roses.

"I told you to call me Levi," he growled. "I have no wish to be the duke."

She could only nod stiffly. "Levi," she whispered softly, which only seemed to agitate him further as he continued to stalk toward her slowly until he was standing right before her.

He reached out with his gloved hand, taking her fingers within his before slowly drawing them toward him, lifting them to his face before planting a kiss on her index finger, right where the rose had pricked her.

A flush of heat began spreading through Siena's veins, from where he touched her to every part of her body as her skin began to tingle with the imagining of what it would be like to feel his lips elsewhere upon her.

"Better?" he asked, his voice rough, and she nodded.

"Better," she tried to reply, only it seemed her voice had disappeared with her senses so heightened.

She tilted her chin up to his searching gaze, her heart thudding against her ribs, each beat resonating through her body. The air around them crackled with tension, the warmth of his breath mingling with hers. The weight of his gaze on her held a magnetic pull that drew her closer to him.

Levi seemed torn between desire and restraint, his hand lingering on hers, the touch sending shivers down her spine. Siena found herself holding her breath, caught in the intensity of the moment.

Without breaking eye contact, Levi slowly traced a finger along her jawline, his touch feather-light yet searing hot against her skin. Siena's heartbeat quickened as she leaned into his touch, a silent plea for more. His thumb brushed against her lower lip, causing her to part them slightly in response.

The world around them seemed to fade away as they stood there in the middle of the woods, enveloped in this well-tended garden that was so at odds with the natural landscape around them.

Without a word, Levi closed the remaining distance between them, capturing her lips in a searing kiss.

The world spun around Siena as his arms encircled her, pulling her closer to his powerful frame. The sensation of his lips moving against hers sent a jolt of electricity through her entire body, igniting a fire within her as she lost herself into him, forgetting who she was as she became one with him instead of two separate people.

Siena's heart pounded in her chest as she allowed herself to be swept away by the moment, forgetting the rest of the world. She ran her fingers through his dark hair, the soft strands entwining with her delicate touch.

Their kiss deepened, becoming more urgent and passionate as they clung to each other under the canopy of the trees above them. Siena felt a sense of freedom she had never experienced before, a liberation from the constraints of society and expectations that had bound her for so long.

As surprisingly as he had kissed her, he released her abruptly, and she nearly fell backward with the intensity of the moment. Siena gasped, her chest rising and falling rapidly as she tried to gather her bearings. Levi stood before her, his gaze intense and unreadable, his own breath ragged.

"Siena," he began, his voice rough with emotion, "I shouldn't have done that."

Confusion tugged at her features as she searched his face for any sign of what he truly felt. "Levi, I—"

But before she could finish, he turned away from her, his

back now facing her. A pang of hurt mixed with longing filled her as she watched him walk a few steps away, clearly battling some inner turmoil.

"Forgive me," he murmured, the words barely audible over the rustling leaves in the quiet glade.

Siena took a hesitant step towards him, her heart aching as the distance between them felt so much greater than it had before he had kissed her.

"There is nothing to forgive," she said. "If I hadn't wanted your touch, then perhaps, but I…"

She floundered, having no experience with such emotion, nor how to put into words what she was feeling. She hardly knew herself. All she knew was that she had enjoyed his touch, craved more of it, and she was surprised by the unexpected surge of anger that ran through her at his denial of what had occurred between them as nothing more than his own relinquishing to a base instinct.

"You have no right to say that to me."

That caught his attention as he whipped around, his cloak billowing about him like a character from a gothic novel.

"Pardon me?"

"If I was able to run away from a marriage that I didn't want, then I would certainly be able to pull back from an embrace if I had no desire for it," she said, as a newfound discovery about herself filled her – that she had the ability to make her own choices, and she wasn't going to allow anyone to take that away from her. "There is nothing to forgive because a kiss that two people wanted is not a mistake, but something to be celebrated."

Her chest was heaving now as she prided herself in her speech, even though it was uncomfortable to make.

"Why would you want to kiss me?" he asked, his voice ragged, his brow furrowed. "I have nothing to offer you."

The realization that he doubted himself more than he doubted her to make her own decision softened her ire, and she took a step closer to him again.

"You have more to offer than you think. You just have to believe it," she said. "Now, tell me about the rose garden."

CHAPTER 11

Levi was still recovering from the shock of their kiss when she asked him about the garden.

How was it that sharing that part of himself made him feel even more vulnerable than the physical closeness between them?

"What is there to tell?" he asked, hoping to deter her, but she continued.

"Why roses?" she asked, and he had to look away from her, off into the distance as he decided whether or not to tell her the full story.

Eventually, he realized that she wasn't going to go away until he explained it in one way or another.

"My mother loved roses," he said, finally. "My brother grew a garden for her, attempting to win her love by giving her the flowers that she adored. I'm not sure whether he succeeded or not, for she wasn't one who would ever say. When our estate burned down, so too did the rose garden."

"So, you planted one here for your mother – or for your brother?"

It was a good question.

"Both, I suppose." He paused, revelling in the strange sensation that here, in this moment, in this grove where the garden lived, he could tell her anything and she wouldn't judge him for it, nor use it against him in some way in the future. "I always thought that the roses were just like my mother – beautiful on the outside, but somewhat prickly when you came too close. I do think, however, that she loved us in her own way. She just didn't know how to show it, didn't know if she was supposed to.

"My brother was the kind of man who didn't care how she treated him – he just wanted to give her that love in whatever way he could. He was the best kind of man there ever was."

"I am sure he would be happy with what you are doing to keep his memory alive," she said quietly, and he noted the tear in her eye from listening to his story.

He swallowed his own emotion.

"He should be here instead of me," he said, his voice raw as he looked in the distance, unable to meet her gaze any longer as the shame ran through him again.

She caught his attention once more when she placed her hand on his arm. "Don't ever say that."

"It's the truth," he said, knowing he was practically glaring at her, but needing her to understand. "Before I became… this, I was not the best of men. I was your typical second son, enjoying life without worrying about the consequences of my actions. Drinking, gambling, womanizing. My brother figured I needed purpose, so he bought me a commission in the army. It was there I became a different man. All thanks to him."

He knew he sounded as though he was feeling sorry for himself, but he needed her to understand.

"Perhaps you are not a different man, but you added more

parts to yourself," she said in that soft, melodic tone of hers, her hand still on his arm as she stared up at him imploringly. "Isn't that who we are? A sum of our experiences? I can tell you that I am not the same woman who agreed to marry Lord Mulberry, but I am not a different woman, either. I have simply grown."

To have grown, not to have changed – he had never thought of it quite like that.

"You are wise beyond your years," he said, unable to fully agree with her and yet appreciating her all the same.

"I like to think I see the parts of themselves that people try to hide," she said. "Why did you plant this out here? Why not in the gardens near the house, where everyone can enjoy?"

"They grow best here," he said, even though it was a lie. It was because near the house, it seemed so exposed, a story that he didn't want to share with anyone, that he never thought he would – until Siena.

She accepted his answer, whether because she understood he didn't want to speak of it or because she believed it, he wasn't certain, but she still crouched beside the rose bush once more.

"Do you think we could pick some flowers for a vase in the house?"

He wanted to say no but then saw the hope on her face and found that he didn't have it within him to deny her.

"For your bedroom," he said, and the smile that lit her face reached right into his heart.

"Thank you," she said. "That would be wonderful."

He pulled out his pocketknife and cut the stems before he took them in hand, not wanting her to prick her finger again. They walked back to the house together at a leisurely pace, Levi leading Lucky.

"How often do you ride?" she asked.

"At least twice a day," he said, catching her surprise. "It gives me the chance to leave the house."

"Do you ever go to London?" she asked.

"No," he said swiftly. "Never."

"You are so close."

He brought a hand to his forehead, running his fingers over his scar. How could she not understand?

"Do you not understand why I would have no wish to be in London?" he asked, hearing the edge to his words but unable to help it. "I am stared at. Ridiculed. Gossiped about. People can barely look at me without flinching. No, London is not for me."

"Not everyone cares about how you look," she said softly. "I don't."

"What do you think then?" he bit out, knowing the truth would hurt but needing to know it regardless.

"I think that you are assuming what other people might think. That you are not giving them a chance."

"I have seen the looks on their faces."

"I can understand why there might be some surprise when people see what has happened to you. But your scars are not who you are but a result of what has happened to you."

"I disagree," he countered.

"I would argue that it is not your scars that keep people away but your cantankerous attitude."

He snorted, even as he knew she was right. It was easier to hide away. It didn't give others the chance to hurt him if he never let them close.

As he inhaled, a scent filled his nose – one that terrified him to the point he wasn't sure if it was truly in the air or if it was part of his nightmarish memory.

"Do you smell that?" he asked her, and she crinkled her

nose most becomingly, distracting him with the way her light freckles added to the aura of sweetness that surrounded her.

"Now that you say it, perhaps I do," she said, looking around. "It smells like—"

That's when there was a huge bang, and they both jumped, Levi immediately tucking Siena behind him as he crouched low, reaching for what was now phantom sword and pistols around his waist.

"Stay behind me," he ordered, as he could sense her trying to see around him one way and then the next.

"I'm sure it is nothing," she said optimistically.

The smell became impossible to ignore the closer they drew to the estate.

Not again.

"Smoke," he muttered, more to himself than Siena, but of course she heard him.

It was swirling in the air around them and he began to panic, the only saving grace was that Siena was here beside him, meaning that she was safe.

"Smoke?" she repeated.

Which meant—

"Fire!"

They heard the call from the stables, and Levi froze so quickly that Siena walked right into the back of him as Lucky's reins slipped out of his hand, although the horse was well enough trained that he stopped a few paces away.

Collins, the stablehand, came running out of the door, leading two horses with him – horses that were throwing their heads in the air as they fought him due to their rising panic as they sensed not only what was chasing them out but also the stablehand's distress.

"Your Grace! You must stay away," he called out, his face dark with soot as sweat ran down his brow from beneath his cap. "The fire is at the back of the stables, but it is spreading quickly."

Levi's pulse was pounding hard as he saw the flames lick the top of the stable roof, heard the cries of the horses inside.

"How many are left?" Siena asked from behind him, although it seemed as though her voice was away in the distance as he was having difficulty focusing on anything but the turmoil within him.

"Five," the stablehand called out as he was already returning to the wooden structure.

Levi knew he should follow him. He had no wish to leave innocent horses to die. And yet, his feet refused to move, as much as he was shouting internally at them to race into the stables and save the horses.

Siena would believe him a coward forever. A scarred, simple coward.

Before he had time to consider the ramifications of that, however, a flash of lilac caught his eye, and it took him a few moments before he realized that Siena had run past him – and was heading right into the stables.

"Siena!" he yelled out. "No!"

This time he didn't give himself any time to think.

He didn't have to tell his feet what to do, because they acted of their own accord, moving toward the stables, chasing after Siena, desperate to stop her before she entered and put herself in danger.

He had just made it to the stable doors when there was a crash from within, and the smoke came billowing out. He came to a halt, as he fought with himself, torn between turning around and running away as fast as he could, and racing inside to save Siena.

Another servant ran by him – a footman, although he couldn't make out which – and Levi felt even more foolish that he couldn't enter to save a woman in his care as well as his own horseflesh.

Him, a soldier. An officer.

"Siena!" he called again, much more desperately this time, and his heart seemed to burst with relief when she reappeared from the smoke, leading one of his horses out, the stablehand following behind with two more and the footman with the last of them.

They all appeared unharmed although were coughing from the smoke. Siena's dress, previously a beautiful lilac, was covered in soot and smudges.

"Your Grace, quickly!" the stablehand said as he urged the horses out in front of him, and as he did so there was a huge crack from within as one of the stable supports must have given out.

Siena's horse bolted into the air, its front legs pawing desperately for support, and Levi finally moved, jumping toward her, wrapping his arms around her and knocking her out of the way and onto the ground as she let go of the reins and the horse ran free.

She landed with an "oof," but Levi took the brunt of the fall.

Wincing in pain, he didn't want to risk them being caught in any further fallout from the fire, and he bent down, ignoring the twinging on his right side as he lifted Siena, throwing her over his shoulder and carrying her away from the stable. When they were a fair distance away, he set her down as gently as he could, crashing to the ground beside her as they watched the flames take over the stable.

"Oh, Levi," she said, a hand over her mouth. "I am so sorry."

He was still catching his breath as the rushing through his veins began to ebb away, leaving him feeling empty and shallow instead.

"You're sorry?" he asked incredulously. "For what?"

"For the loss of your stable," she said. "Are you all right?"

Her eyes ran over him, and he could tell that she was not asking about his physical ailments, for *she* was the one who had entered the stables, who had put herself in danger, and saved a horse who wouldn't have otherwise made it.

Never before had he felt like less of a man.

And that was saying something.

CHAPTER 12

Siena wasn't sure if it was her words that distressed him or the burning stable.

Perhaps both.

But she certainly wasn't helping.

They sat there together in the overgrown grass, watching flames lick at the wooden walls of the stable while black smoke billowed out into the air, the smell of burnt hay and smoke mixed with the sharp tang of wet wood and the musky scent of the horses blanketing them.

Just when it appeared the fire was threatening to spread, however, it seemed to quickly die out, struggling to catch on the wet wood of the stable's exterior. Being contained to the flammable contents inside muffled the crackling of the fire, creating a dampened and almost eerie sound.

The servants had arrived with buckets, but they weren't needed. The rain from the previous days had done its job and stifled the fire – although not before destroying the stable. Most of it stood, but Siena guessed it would have to be torn down and rebuilt.

Levi stood before Siena could ask anything further, his

breeches soaked through from sitting on the damp ground. He held out his left hand to assist her. She took it, the warmth of his touch rushing through her.

With everyone now safe and the fire contained, Siena had the chance to mull over Levi's reaction when they had discovered the fire. The look on his face had been one of pure terror as his entire body had rigidly stood in one place.

That was panic if she had ever seen it. It was how she had felt on her wedding day, knowing what awaited her.

If it hadn't been for Eliza, she never would have found her way out of it.

Which was why she was determined to be there for Levi. To help him come to terms with the event that had scarred him and had turned him into a shell of the man he used to be. She could see it within him, knew there was more to him that was struggling to come out, that he wouldn't allow a voice.

The tenseness remained between them as they walked through the front door of the house together. An air of emptiness surrounded them as all of the servants had vacated to see to the fire – even the maids had likely been filling buckets and adding their assistance wherever possible.

Siena and Levi said nothing to one another as they climbed the stairs, taking the same turn at the landing as his bedroom was at the end of the wing where hers was located.

She paused in front of her door, waiting for him to stop, to say anything, but his steps continued down the corridor as he didn't even look back at her.

"Levi?"

She didn't know why she had called to him – she just knew that she didn't want him to go. It was the first time she had called him by his first name without his prompting, and somehow it felt right. He might be a duke, but here, on this estate with just the two of them alone, they were Levi and

Siena, two people who had found one another at a time when they both needed comfort.

"Are you truly well?" he asked, concern crossing his face. "Or were you injured?"

"I am well, although I fear my throat might ache for a few days from the smoke," she said. "Would you like to… come in?"

She waved toward her bedchamber, and she saw the hesitation on his face. She wasn't sure if it was because of the kiss they had shared or his reaction to the stable fire, but he seemed rather ill at ease.

"I won't bite. I promise," she said, attempting to inject some humor into the situation, but he didn't seem to notice. "I suppose I was just hoping for some company after our ordeal."

It was true, she realized. She didn't want to be alone. But even more than that, she sensed that he needed someone, and it surprised her how much she wanted to be that person for him.

"Very well," he said, walking by her stiffly.

"I suppose I shall need a bath, although I do not want to bother the maids, not with everything else they are busy with," she said, which caused him to stand and walk to the door, and she held up a hand before he could do what he was likely planning and call for help for her. "No, please do not ask them."

"Their first priority should be to see to your comfort."

"I am fine. Truly," she said. "Nothing that I cannot see to myself."

She walked over to the washbasin in the corner, pouring water into the bowl before dipping linen into it and wiping her face, trying to rid it of the soot that had covered it when she had entered the stable.

Entering the stables had terrified her, and yet she had

acted without thinking, focused on one purpose only — saving the horses. She hadn't realized how affected Levi had been until she had come out the other side.

Levi was now standing awkwardly in the middle of the room, so Siena walked over to the bed and sat down on the end of it before patting the mattress beside her.

"Come sit," she said, although he didn't move. "Please?" she added, and finally, with a terse nod, he did, the limp on his left side obvious.

"Did you hurt yourself when you prevented the horse from hitting me?" she asked, and his lips drew tightly together. She had thought the big horse was going to knock her over with one of those large hooves of his when he had risen up in panic, but then Levi had saved her. Again.

"I'm fine."

"You do not always have to be fine, you know," she said, to which he gave a snort of derision.

"Oh, I am far from fine. I am always far from fine. That is the very problem."

He said it with such passion that Siena knew she should be upset, but she had a feeling that it had nothing to do with her. Rather, it was emotion he was finally releasing.

She leaned in toward him, watching his expression.

"Levi, what happened?"

"I didn't do what I should have done. You are the last person who should have been saving those horses. That was my job. I am not only the lord of this manor and all that reside within it – people and animal alike – but I have been trained to protect those around me, not to put them in further danger."

"I am not speaking about what happened today," she clarified, "although I should note that this is the third time you saved me – the first from the highwaymen, the second in the library when I fell from the ladder. I would say that you have proven yourself to be a rather adept protector. But what I am wondering is what happened in your past that has caused you to be so terrified of fire? I know that you *wanted* to go into the stables today, but something prevented you from doing so. Your scars look like burns to me. Did it happen during the war? Or were you there when your home burned down?"

"Are you trying to gather gossip so that you can add to the fodder about me?"

She allowed his acidic words to slide off of her, knowing that he didn't mean them – not against her.

"We both know that I am not returning to London anytime soon," she said, meeting his eye and arching a brow. "Nor am I one to add to any gossip. I sense, however, that you have never spoken about what happened to you and I think, perhaps, it is time that you did so. Now, tell me. What has you so afraid?"

* * *

Levi lowered his head, resting his face in his hands, unable to look at her any longer. She was right. He had never spoken about it. Fitz knew the particulars, but most of it he had gathered from servants who had shared some of the facts of the day with him.

She was so intent on labelling him this savior figure. However, he wondered if he should tell her the truth – maybe then she would understand that he didn't deserve any of the accolades or compliments she sent his way.

"You know that I was in the army," he said, his mind leaving the room they were in, this conversation between them, and heading back years in time but felt like another lifetime entirely. "I was an officer, of course, my brother having purchased my commission, as I told you. When I entered the war, I was doubtful, resentful, wanting to return to the life that I had left."

He stood now, hands in his pockets as he walked away from the bed and stared out the window at the land before him, the sky as grey and cloudy as his mood. Guilt washed over him at the emotions he had held toward the brother who had only wanted what was best for him.

"Over time, I began to... not necessarily enjoy what I was doing but I did lean into the purpose it had provided me. I learned what I was capable of as I became responsible and protective of those who were under my leadership."

That part of the story was the easy part to tell. It was what came next that he struggled with.

"My father died ten years ago, and my brother, who was five years my senior, became a tremendous duke. He was the man who every woman wanted and every other man wanted to be. He was prepared to marry the jewel of the season, although the two of them did seem rather ill-matched. He had the lands in order, the house at its peak. He was a stand-up member of Parliament, never missing a session, always ready to attend any function required of him. My mother had been so proud of him before she died." He paused for a moment, remembering how he had never felt that he could measure up, that he was always lacking in some way, which was why he had tried to be someone else instead of a shadow of his brother.

"It was her funeral which brought me home. I was on leave, at our family estate. I am sure you heard what happened. There was a fire. I was out on a ride when it broke out in the kitchen. It should have been contained there, but there was so much happening throughout the home that there was much to catch flame. The structure was stone, but the fire was strong and ripped through the areas we so commonly used – kitchen, dining room, drawing room.

"I returned right when my brother was preparing to enter. I wanted to see to our safety, but my brother said he was the leader of the estate, and he should be the one to make sure that no one was left behind. He entered the kitchen to save a scullery maid who had become trapped behind a table. Just as he was leading her out the door, a timber fell on top of him, crushing him, although somehow, he managed to push the maid out of harm's way."

A choked sob emerged from Siena, and he closed his eye at the pain that remained, that was resurfacing from this telling.

"I tried to lift it off of him, truly I did. But it was wedged in tightly and was far too heavy to even budge. From what I'm told, eventually the fire overtook me. It was burning my clothes when one of the footmen pulled me off of my brother and managed to put out the flames upon me, although it left its mark."

He didn't know she had moved behind him until her hands pressed softly around his waist. Before he knew what was happening, she was resting her head against his back, her arms wrapping around him.

"By the time they put out the fire, my brother was gone. Burned. They thought I was going to die as well, and I should have."

He turned around to face her fully, pushing away her arms, needing her to understand that he didn't deserve this from her.

"It should have been me who died instead."

CHAPTER 13

Siena's breath caught in her throat, her heart breaking at the pain that dripped from Levi's words. His shoulders tensed as he stepped back from her and pushed her away.

She had known his story would be difficult, but she had never expected just how raw and emotional it would be. Anguish washed over his face as the guilt practically seeped out of him. Siena reached out a trembling hand, cupping his cheek gently, her voice barely above a whisper.

"Levi, you can't blame yourself for what happened. It was a tragedy, an accident... you did everything you could to save him. More than most people ever would," she implored, her eyes pleading with him to see the truth in her words.

Levi closed his eye, his jaw clenched tight, and Siena could only imagine the flood of memories that sharing had brought up. He had carried this burden for so long that the weight must have been crushing him.

Siena took a chance and stepped in toward him, staring up at him earnestly, needing him to know that all hope was not lost.

"You don't understand, Siena," he murmured hoarsely, his hands trembling at his sides. "I failed him in the worst way. He was a good man. Such a better man than I. What was the point of it all?"

"I wish I knew," she said, reaching up and lifting her hands to his face, feeling the puckered scars beneath her fingers, knowing how much the burns still pained him. What must it be like to walk around with a constant reminder of the worst moment of your life? "What I do know is that if he was as good of a man as you say he was, then he wouldn't want you to live like this. Alone. Shut off from the world on this estate, pushing everyone away from you. What would he want you to be doing?"

"Being a good duke, I suppose," he muttered, his good eye catching hers.

"But in your own way," she said earnestly. "You cannot *be* him. You are not the same person. But you can be the best version of yourself."

"I am not sure there is a best version."

Siena lifted her chin, unwavering in her conviction as she stared into his stormy face. "I beg to differ. I have seen glimpses of the man you truly are, Levi. Beneath the walls you have built around yourself using your scars and your burdens lies a kind-hearted, honorable man. You may not see it now, but I do."

Levi's gaze softened at her words, a flicker of something akin to hope dancing in his eyes. Siena took a step closer, her hand reaching out to grasp his tightly.

"Let me show you the man I see," she whispered, her voice unwavering with determination. "You don't have to face this alone anymore."

For a moment, silence hung heavy between them, the weight of their shared emotions palpable in the air. Then, Levi let out a shaky breath, and Siena nearly cried as she could see him beginning to peek out around the corner of his walls.

"I never expected to find someone like you," he admitted quietly. "Someone who sees beyond the darkness that haunts me. Who isn't afraid to look at me."

Siena's heart swelled with newfound courage as she stepped closer to him, their faces only inches apart. The warmth of his breath mingled with hers, the electric tension crackling between them as they stood on the precipice of something unknown yet all too tantalizing.

Levi's hand trembled slightly as he reached up to brush a stray strand of hair away from Siena's face, his touch gentle yet charged with an unspoken desire. His eye searched hers, a silent question hanging in the air - was she sure about this?

Without uttering a word, Siena closed the remaining distance between them, her lips meeting his in a tentative yet achingly sweet kiss. It was as if time stood still in that moment, the weight of their shared burdens lifting ever so slightly as their hearts found solace in each other's embrace.

Levi responded fervently, his arms encircling her waist as he deepened the kiss, and Siena could practically taste all of his pent-up longing pouring through his touch.

As they kissed, a flood of emotions rushed through Siena - relief, desire, and a newfound sense of connection that she had never expected to find with anyone, least of all this reclusive duke. Siena could feel Levi's hesitations melt away as he kissed her with a hunger that spoke volumes about the depth of his feelings.

When they finally broke apart, both were breathless, their gazes locked in a silent exchange of unspoken promises. Siena could see a mix of emotions swirling in Levi's face - gratitude, longing, and a hint of fear.

Levi's thumb gently traced her cheekbone as he whispered hoarsely, "I do not deserve you, Siena. I am broken and scarred, inside and out."

Siena placed a finger over his lips, silencing his doubts. "You are worthy of love, Levi. Your scars do not define you; they are a testament to the battles you've fought and survived. You deserve happiness as much as anyone."

And she was about to show him exactly what she meant.

* * *

Levi's heart thundered in his chest as Siena's words echoed in his mind, her touch a balm to his wounded soul. He closed his eyes, drowning in the scent of her hair, the warmth of her body so close to his. When she traced her fingers over the rough texture of his scars on his cheek and neck, a shiver ran down his spine.

He should stop her — to continue would be more than he should allow, for more reasons than one. She was a proper young lady, too beautiful, too tender, too innocent for a man like him.

But it was the first time in the longest time that he could remember feeling at peace, loved, as more than the scarred duke about whom rumors abounded. He would do anything to take care of her, to protect her.

And right now, maybe he would do so by just being in the moment.

With her.

With utmost tenderness, Siena began to undress him, each piece of fabric falling away like barriers between them.

Levi's breath caught in his throat as Siena's hands moved with purpose, undoing the buttons of his shirt one by one. His heart raced with a heady mix of desire and vulnerability as she bared his chest, revealing the network of scars that crisscrossed his skin.

Siena's touch was gentle yet sure as she traced each scar with her fingertips, her lips following in their wake to leave soft, reassuring kisses in their path. Levi closed his eyes, overwhelmed by the rush of emotions coursing through him - disbelief that someone could look at him with such tenderness, longing for the connection he had denied himself for fear of rejection, and a flicker of hope that maybe, just maybe, he could let himself be loved.

When she finally met his gaze, Levi saw nothing but acceptance, and, he realized, hunger, which only made his own need for her all the more encompassing.

As her hands moved lower, undoing his trousers with a confidence that both thrilled and terrified him, Levi's resolve wavered. He wanted her with a desperation that bordered on madness, but he also feared the depth of emotion she stirred within him. She was a beacon of light in his darkened world, a reminder of everything he had denied himself for far too long.

Yet Levi could no longer ignore the primal urge that pulsed through him and with a low growl, he pulled Siena close, their bodies melding together as if they were made to fit perfectly against one another.

Levi barely even registered the fire crackling in the hearth, which would normally have his every nerve on edge with fear.

Instead, he noticed how the flickering light cast a warm glow, accentuating the curves of Siena's body above him.

Her hands roamed over Levi's skin, and he captured her lips in a searing kiss, pouring all his longing and desire into it. Their breath mingled, hearts pounding in unison as they gave in to the pull between them.

"Time to be rid of this," he said, reaching up and grasping the material of her ruined dress on either side of the buttons that ran up the back of it. Seeing no reason to take care of a garment that would have to be disposed of anyway, he ripped it down the back, the small buttons jumping away from their seams to dance over the bed and along the floor. Siena's eyes glazed over at his show of force, and a surge of strength rushed through him that he could still cause such a reaction in a woman.

Siena slid the rest of her dress off her body, followed by her chemise and stays until she was as bare as he was, and he stilled for a moment as he ran his gaze over her, struck by her beauty and the fact that she was here with him, had chosen him, wanted him.

Levi's large, possessive hands moved with a reverent urgency, exploring every inch of Siena's body as if committing each moment to memory. Her skin was soft against his rough palms, her gasps of pleasure urging him on.

"Levi," Siena whispered his name like a prayer, her voice husky with need.

He groaned in response, his own desire reaching a fever pitch as he felt her heat against him. He needed to be inside her, to feel her surround him, to make her his — even if it was just for tonight.

He pushed himself off the bed, no longer content to be beneath her as a part of his former self returned, the raw, masculine piece that could no longer lie passively but needed to take action and show this woman his strength.

Siena's eyes widened in surprise and desire as she arched beneath him in a silent plea for more.

When he met her gaze, he saw the naked emotion swirling within her eyes. The desire and trust mirrored back at him was more intoxicating than any whiskey he'd ever tasted, more addictive than any card game he'd ever partaken in.

"I want you, Siena," he growled, his voice low and gravelly

with need. She nodded, her gaze never leaving his, and whispered, "Take me."

With fierce intensity that belied their tender connection, Levi positioned himself at her entrance, his eyes locked on hers as he entered her slowly, savoring the feel of her warm, wet core surrounding him.

Siena moaned softly, her legs wrapping around his waist as she pulled him closer, her nails digging into his shoulders as their bodies moved in perfect harmony. Their kiss deepened, their tongues entwined as they sought comfort and strength in each other's embrace. Levi thrust deeper, his rhythm matching the erratic pounding of his heart. Siena met each thrust, her hips rocking in response, driving them both higher and higher.

Their cries echoed around the room, as Levi couldn't help but be lost in the feeling of Siena, her velvety skin squeezing him as he moved within her. Her breathing was ragged, her pleas for mercy and desire intertwined.

In that moment, he knew he was lost. Lost in Siena, lost in this unholy pleasure, lost in the raw and primitive need to claim her. He had fought to deny her but forces greater than him had quelled any chance of that.

For she was stronger than she seemed, stronger than she likely even knew herself.

And if she didn't know it yet, then he would make sure that she understood, from this moment on.

"Levi!" she cried as she began to pulse around him, and he lost himself in her, pumping hard until the very last moment when he forced himself to pull out of her and spend on the sheets beside her.

He returned to her, holding himself up on his elbows above her, their noses touching as they breathed deeply, lost in one another and the moment that had overtaken them.

He should not have taken her innocence.

But he would worry about that later.

For now, he would clean her up and treat her like the priceless woman she was.

She had forever buried herself inside his heart.

The only problem was that he had no idea how he would ever let her go.

CHAPTER 14

The woman Siena had been but a few weeks ago would never believe what she had just done.

She was not, however, the same woman anymore.

Nor did she want to go back.

As she and Levi lay together, wrapped up in the blankets and this moment, she couldn't help but wonder how it was possible to so completely begin to understand herself while at the same time becoming so immersed in who the two of them were together.

She reached up, running her hands up and down Levi's back as she held him against her, her heart swelling at how he had opened up to her while at the same time shown her a side of himself that she hadn't expected – one that was primal, powerful, and possessive in a way that thrilled her.

"You are incredible," she whispered, their breath still intermingling. "That was utterly unbelievable."

"Happy to hear it," he said. "But it is you that takes my breath away."

They lay there, revelling in one another, where they likely could have been lost together all day, until there was a knock at the door, and they both started, suddenly coming back to the present.

In their discovery of one another, they had almost forgotten all of the turmoil that had brought them to this moment and the destruction that lay beyond these doors.

"My lady?" came Mary's distressed voice. "Are you there? Are you well? We couldn't find you and—"

"I am fine, Mary!" Siena called out. "Please, give me a moment to collect myself and then perhaps a bath would be lovely."

"Very well, my lady," Mary responded in relief as well as some confusion, but her footsteps soon faded down the hall.

Levi looked down at Siena, one corner of his mouth uplifted in amusement as he reached out and brushed his thumb over her cheek.

"You missed some soot," he said, although his smile quickly fled as he was also apparently brought back to the terror from earlier.

"Thank you," she said quietly, earnestly, and his brow furrowed in confusion.

"For what?"

"For sharing with me. For helping me understand who you are."

"Mine is not a happy story," he said, his hands twisted in the blankets beneath him. "It's also one that many people meet with suspicion."

"Because they believe that you started the fire," she said, repeating the rumors she had heard time and again.

"You have read the scandal sheets."

"I have, and they are nothing but that – scandalous papers that will do anything to make a sale. I know that you had nothing to do with that fire, and that if you could, you would go back in time and stop it from ever occurring."

"Thank you," he said, reaching out and covering one of her hands with his own.

"For what?"

"For trusting me. Believing in me."

"It's the truth," she said simply, pausing for a moment before asking, "how did the fire start?"

"That is where the rumors began," he said, throwing himself back down on the bed, "for signs pointed to the potential of the fire being started deliberately. There was an abundance of oil in the kitchen and a few of the servants identified a person fleeing from the area at the time."

"None of that should lead anyone to believe that it was you."

"It shouldn't," he said grimly. "But people can be quick to turn one small fact into a much bigger story. I am sorry to share all of this melancholy with you."

"Don't be. It is your story," she said, reaching out and pushing his hair, which had grown far too long for the style of the day but suited him, away from his face. "When I told you that we will face it together, those were not just words."

He nodded, the trust on his face causing her heart to swell.

"I suppose we best get you cleaned up so that we do not scandalize Mary," he said, reluctantly lifting himself off her.

"I have a feeling that your staff would be quite pleased to know that you are happy," she said as she crossed the room, finding her wrapper and slipping it over her shoulders.

He nodded as though he were about to say something, scratching his head, telling that he was just realizing what their coming together likely meant for her and their future.

Enough emotions had arisen today already, though, and Siena worried that having to make any further decisions would be altogether too much.

That could come another day.

"You should go before the bath arrives," she said. "I know we are both scandalous already in our own way, but—"

"This might be too much, even for us," he said with a small, slightly relieved smile as he dressed before crossing to her, leaning down, and placing the sweetest, most caring kiss on her lips.

It was one she would carry with her until they were together like this again.

Which she hoped would be very soon.

* * *

Buoyed by Siena, Levi carried the bliss of their encounter through the rest of the day as he faced the destroyed stable and directed his staff to find makeshift shelter for the horses in the barn until they could rebuild enough of the stable to make them comfortable once more.

Levi stood beside Collins, the stablemaster, as they watched the footmen help lead the horses away while the smoke still trickled up from the burned building.

"I must apologize, Your Grace," Collins said, rubbing his forehead, which was thickly streaked with soot. "I have no idea how the fire started. There was enough light from the windows that we didn't have any lanterns lit, and as far as I know, no one was smoking inside. I shall have to ask and see if anyone can think of a cause, but—"

"It's not your fault, Collins," Levi said, stopping him and then catching the stablemaster's surprised expression. Levi supposed that his staff was not accustomed to him being so forgiving, but he was in a different mood than usual today.

"Once the smoke clears and the embers burn out and we can go inside, I'm sure we can determine what happened, but it will only be to prevent it from taking place again. No blame will be laid." Levi pursed his lips together, deciding that he'd had more than enough experience with fires than most people should ever have.

He clapped the stablemaster on the shoulder and was returning to the house when McGregor caught up to him.

"Your Grace," he said with a nod, as he always referred to him by his proper title when they were in public settings. "How are you doing? I can imagine that the fire must have been very traumatic for you."

"It was, in a way, yes," he said, letting out a breath. "It brought back memories that I would prefer to leave in the past. At least, however, no one was hurt."

"I heard Lady Siena was rather close."

"Yes," Levi said, rubbing his forehead as he tried to push the new memory away as well. "Far too close." McGregor appeared troubled, and Levi remembered then that he was not the only one involved in a previous fire. McGregor had lost his own father – a baker – to a fire, and then had witnessed the same fire Levi had endured.

"This must be difficult for you as well, McGregor."

"Never mind me," the valet said, but before Levi could ask anything further, he squinted when he saw a line of people walking around the building and flinched in response, although he didn't run – not yet.

It took him a moment to realize that not all of the people around the barn and stables were his staff, but rather people he had never seen before. An uneasy ball began to roll around his stomach, although he wasn't nearly as on edge as he usually was at the thought of someone seeing him for the first time. He supposed it was because he was used to it at this point and no matter what the people here thought, he was still their duke.

"Who are these people? I do not recognize many of them."

"They are tenants from nearby as well as people from the town," McGregor explained. "They have come to see what they can do to help. There is already talk of coming together to build a new stable."

"How much would I pay them for that?" he asked.

"They would never agree to take payment," Thornbury said, joining them. "This is what they do – help one another in times of need."

Levi was already shaking his head as he took some steps back. For one, he didn't want to allow anyone to take a close look at his face. He wasn't sure that he could stand that kind of scrutiny at the moment, especially not after he was beginning to hope that maybe if Siena could handle what he looked like, others might be able to see past his visage as well.

He couldn't have those hopes dashed.

Not today.

* * *

SIENA HAD SPENT the rest of the day after the fire by herself. By the time she had finished her bath, evening had already descended, and Siena readied for bed and took dinner in her chamber, as exhaustion had set in from the events of the day – the terror of the fire and the elation with Levi that followed.

She had hoped that he hadn't waited for her for dinner, but Mary had informed her that he had been so busy with the staff as they looked after the horses and stable that he had missed dinner altogether. Siena wasn't keen on that news, but she supposed that he was a grown man and didn't need her to tell him when to eat or not.

She hadn't seen him at all the next day either, although she had spied him through the windows from time to time. She had been very pleased when she had received a message from him, telling her that he looked forward to seeing her at dinner that night.

This meant that now she was looking rather forlornly at her wardrobe, devoid of her favorite of the gowns Eliza had packed for her now that it was ruined. None of the rest seemed to be appropriate for this evening.

At some point, she was going to have to buy new dresses, although she wasn't certain how to do so when she had no wish to return to London and she doubted that Levi would welcome a seamstress into his home.

Which was why she was greatly surprised when Mary knocked on the door and walked in with her arms full of beautiful golden fabric.

"What's this?" Siena asked as Mary practically beamed while laying out what appeared to be a gown upon the bed.

"The duke asked that I bring this to you to wear tonight."

"Where is it from?" she asked as she brought a hand to her throat, aghast at the beauty of the gown. From its style, she guessed that it was created decades ago, but still, it didn't appear worn, and it practically glittered in the candlelight.

"I have never seen it before myself, but perhaps the duke can provide you with an explanation," Mary said, as she busied herself helping Siena prepare for dinner.

Siena walked over, stroking her hands over the beautiful silk.

"What is it for? It is far too extravagant for a simple dinner, is it not?"

Mary smiled coyly. "The Cook told me that His Grace asked her to prepare a special dinner tonight."

"For how many people?" Siena asked, wondering if he had invited guests – perhaps this friend Fitz she had heard of.

"Just the two of you," Mary answered, giving her eyebrows a quick wiggle that had Siena laughing even as her heart fluttered slightly.

A dinner shouldn't seem particularly important after what had happened between them yesterday, and yet… if he was putting an effort into doing something for her, perhaps that meant that he actually cared.

She couldn't help her giggle of excitement and clapped her hand over her mouth after she allowed it to escape, but Mary held no judgement. In fact, it seemed that the maid shared her enthusiasm as she flitted about the room even faster while she carefully helped Siena with her hair and a bit of rouge on her cheeks. Siena wished she had a few jewels to match the beautiful gown, but its finery would have to do.

Soon enough she was prepared, standing in front of the mirror, facing Mary.

"Well?" she said, taking the fabric of the dress between her thumb and forefinger as she lifted it out to the sides. "What do you think?"

"You are stunning," Mary said with a sigh of contentment. "Absolutely beautiful. I can see why the duke is falling for you."

"Falling for me?" Siena said, her mouth gaping open. "I am not sure I would call it that."

"The man has barely left his bedchamber or his study since he arrived here over a year ago, and I have only ever heard him speak to Thornbury or McGregor. Even then, he practically grunted his words. But today, even after the stable nearly burned down, I saw him *smile*. Lady Siena, I have not seen that man smile once in all my time working here. That is because of you."

"Perhaps he just needed some company," Siena said somewhat bashfully. She had hoped to help the duke find a reversal of his spirit, a lightness that had previously been absent, but she could hardly imagine that he would see her as more than that, that there might even be potential for him to fall in *love* with her.

Love. She had never imagined that it might be in her

future – most especially with a man like the Duke of Dunmore.

After Mary's approval, she took a breath and opened the door to face whatever surprise awaited her with her stomach in knots – but happy, excited knots.

Siena walked toward the stairs with some trepidation, finding that her fingers were shaking on the banister. She stood at the top, wondering just where she was supposed to meet the duke, what he might have waiting for her, why he was doing this – and then she saw him.

He was standing at the bottom of the staircase, more dapper than she had ever seen him before. He wore trousers and a jacket of rich, dark velvet, his waistcoat adorned with intricate gold embroidery and shiny buttons that matched her gown.

Even his cravat had obviously been carefully selected, starched, and tied, his eye patch made of new black silk, and her heart swelled that he had gone to such effort for her.

"Lady Siena," he said, his voice nearly cracking as he held out a hand toward her. "I've been waiting for you."

CHAPTER 15

Levi had nearly forgotten how to speak when Siena had appeared at the top of the stairs.

She was a vision in gold, illuminating the darkness of the house – darkness brought upon by the lack of lit wall sconces or fire in the hearths, darkness that he had brought with him when he had made this his home.

But now that she was here, everything had changed.

His voice had nearly failed him when he had finally greeted her, so affected he was by her, but she didn't seem to care so then, neither did he. He wore gloves but, strangely, for the first time since the accident, he had an intense desire to remove them, if only to feel the touch of her skin beneath his.

"You are very handsome tonight," she said as she slipped her small hand into his, and he curled his fingers around hers, knowing she was only being polite but accepting the compliment all the same.

"And you," he said, pausing as he ran his eyes up and down her figure, "are stunning."

The blush of her cheeks deepened.

"Where did you find this gown?"

"When I moved here, I had my servants look through all of the items that had been stored away. I gave away many of them, but something made me hold onto this," he said. "I'm glad I did."

He led her across the foyer and into the dining room, where he had asked the staff to prepare a table worthy of her.

Her gasp when she entered was well worth their efforts.

"What is all of this?" she asked as he held out her chair next to his at the head of the table, pushing her in.

"You said you loved the roses," he said, as they both admired the petals splayed out upon the table, the flowers cut and placed into vases.

"Yes, but you didn't have to cut them for me," she said, meeting his gaze. "I would have been just as happy to return to the garden to see them."

"Which we can do as well," he said, surprising himself by reaching out and plucking a flower off of the table before placing it in her hair, slipping one of the pins around it as it contrasted perfectly with her fair strands. "Beautiful," he said, admiring her.

"Why are you doing all of this?" she asked, spreading her hands out in front of her. "It is absolutely lovely, and I do appreciate it, but I am happy to simply have dinner with you."

He reached out, taking her hand in his again. He liked it there. It fit.

"You deserve so much, Siena. Ballrooms where you are announced at the top of the stairs and all eyes in the room turn upon you. Lavish estates. A beautiful London townhouse. To be the talk of the *ton* because of how stunning you are. I cannot give you all of that. But I can give you this. So let me."

She dipped her head before shifting her chair ever closer to his.

"Here is the thing – I do not want all that. I am the talk of the *ton* now and I have no desire for it. I could have had the estates and the townhouse and the riches. But all I ever wanted was to find love."

The word hung in the air between them, although both of them appeared too hesitant to remark upon it any further.

Just when Levi felt the need to say more, the doors to the dining room opened and in came Thornbury himself, obviously quite pleased with the entire setting.

"Your Grace. My lady. I am ever so pleased to present your first course."

Levi had to hide his smile at the man's theatrics. It appeared that the last year of no guests – at least, none who were invited – had starved the man of the opportunity to host.

"Thank you, Thornbury," Siena said, providing him with the smile that Levi had come to thrive upon. "Please tell all who decorated this room that it is ever so lovely."

"Of course. They will be most pleased at your praise," he said before leaving.

"This is delicious," Siena said upon trying the soup, surprised, and Levi smiled to himself. The Cook had outdone herself. He knew she had grown tired of cooking for him alone, but it seemed Siena's arrival had revived her spirits – as it had for most of the staff.

He cleared his throat.

"Siena." He was more serious now, uncertain of how to broach the subject. He was becoming used to her being here and had no wish for her to leave, but he knew that he couldn't keep her here forever as though she was his prisoner in this tower that he never left. "The roads will be dry in but a day or two and as much as I would absolutely love to have you stay here with me, it is not exactly… proper."

She paused for just a moment before she laughed a high, tinkling laugh. "Levi. After yesterday, what difference does propriety make? No one knows that I am here. And even if they did, you and I are not exactly above scandal, now, are we?"

He had to chuckle ruefully. "I suppose we are not."

She sobered slightly. "If you want me to leave, I understand. But if you want me to stay… then I am happy to stay for as long as we both wish it."

Warmth began to bloom in his heart, that she was not running away, but also hadn't put any pressure of permanence upon him.

For it was not that he didn't want her forever – he just had a feeling that eventually the novelty would wear off and she would want to return to her old life. He was willing to endure the heartbreak that would bring with it.

As long as he could have her for now.

* * *

Siena could hardly believe that this man sitting in front of her was the same one she had encountered just a week ago. He was not exactly enigmatic, but a glimmer of a man who cared had come shining through.

"I must ask you something," she said, her fingers playing over the stem of her glass. They had enjoyed five courses, and she couldn't eat another bite, but nor did she want this evening with him to end.

"Ask me anything you'd like," he said, splaying his hands out in front of her, and she appreciated that he would provide her such an opportunity.

"Anything?" she said, wondering if he truly meant it.

"Yes."

"Very well," she said, but now that she had her chance, shyness took over. "Have you… ever done anything like this for a woman before?"

"What do you mean?"

"This dinner. The effort you have put in tonight to make me feel special. Is this how you used to court women?"

He stared her directly in the eye as he slowly shook his head. "Never."

"Never?"

"No. I will not lie and say that there were never other women, but none of them were special. Not like you."

Siena had to bite her lip to hide the smile that threatened to bloom far too big at his response and she dipped her head so that she wouldn't look like a lovesick fool.

But then he reached out, his forefinger catching her beneath her chin as he raised her face to look at him again.

"My turn to ask you a question."

She turned serious once more.

"Of course."

"Why were you not scared of me when you first arrived? Why did you not hide from me or run away in fear?"

"A person's visage does not scare me. I have seen far too many people who were beautiful, flawless, even, on the outside, but most atrocious underneath."

"You are different from anyone I've ever met," he said, pausing for a moment to simply look at her, and she warmed under his scrutiny. "I was as horrible to you as I am to anyone else. You should have wanted to run from here. From me. Why didn't you?"

"Well, for one, the roads were impassable," she said, jesting, although she only received a half smile in response. "But truly, Levi, when you saved me, I saw a protective, heroic side in you. You could have easily continued riding and pretended that you never saw me. But you didn't, despite the fact that you wanted nothing more than to be left alone where no one could find you. That showed me that perhaps there was more to you than you showed others, and if I only dug a little deeper, I would like what I found."

"And did you?" he asked, his voice nearly a whisper.

"I most certainly did," she said, barely able to finish her breathless response before he leaned in and his mouth crashed upon hers, his thirst for her and depth of his emotion present in his kiss.

Siena would have loved to progress this kiss, to sit on his lap with his strong arms wrapped around her back, but their current positions allowed nothing more than their lip lock. When he finally pulled back, they were both breathless, staring at one another, wondering just where this night was going to take them.

It seemed, however, that he had an idea.

"Do you like to dance?"

"I do," she said, surprised when he stood and held out a hand toward her. She took his offer and followed him through the doors to the drawing room, although she couldn't help but look around in confusion. "We do not have anyone to play music for us."

"On that, you are wrong," he said before raising his voice ever so slightly. "Mrs. Porter?"

Siena had to place a hand over her mouth which gaped open in astonishment as the housekeeper entered the room with a wide smile on her face and bustled over to the pianoforte, sitting down before it.

"When I discovered that our esteemed housekeeper plays for the staff many evenings, I could not help but ask her to play for us," he said, before nodding to Mrs. Porter, who began the first few notes of a pleasant song that Siena found somewhat familiar, although she couldn't quite place it.

"Shall we?" he said to Siena, holding his arms out, and she stepped into them as though they had been molded as one figurine, broken apart only to come together once more.

Mrs. Porter was more than adept on the keys, but that was not what most shocked Siena.

It was when Levi opened his mouth and began to sing.

"Where the bee sucks, there suck I;

In a cowslip's bell I lie:

There I couch when owls do cry.

On the bat's back I do fly

After summer merrily.

Merrily, merrily, shall I live now,

Under the blossom that hangs on the bough."'

If he hadn't been leading her, Siena was fairly certain that she would have stopped dancing entirely, transfixed by him.

"Levi," she said as he came to a close. "Your voice... is magnificent."

It was his turn to blush as he murmured, "Thank you."

"Shakespeare," she said, recognizing the song. *"The Tempest.* That's very romantic."

"You bring out the romantic in me, I suppose," he said as his gaze remained intent on her while he gripped her in his embrace, leading her around the room.

Siena felt like she was floating on air as they danced, her hand in Levi's strong grasp, her gaze locked with his. The melody woven by Mrs. Porter filled the room, swirling around them like an enchantment.

They moved gracefully across the floor, Levi's steps as sure and as fluid as when he rode Lucky. His presence was commanding yet gentle, his eye sparkling with a warmth that melted her defenses.

The way Levi sang those lines from Shakespeare's play made Siena's heart ache with longing. His voice carried a depth of emotion that resonated with her soul as if he were baring his heart to her through the lyrics. She was falling deeper under his spell, drawn to him in a way she couldn't quite comprehend.

She knew she was being selfish, that at some point she would have to leave this sanctuary and find a new direction.

But she would give anything to be lost in this moment forever.

CHAPTER 16

When the last notes of the song came to an end, Levi held Siena's hand up between them, placing a kiss upon it before bowing to her and she sank into a deep curtsy, the gold of her dress shimmering in the dimly lit room.

He had become accustomed to small fires in the grate – he'd had no choice, or else he would freeze to death – but he felt more at ease than he had been in quite some time with Siena's presence.

"Well, Lady Siena," he said, grinning at her mischievously. "You must be tired. I will walk you to your chamber."

"I would appreciate that," she said, a spark in her eyes that matched his playfulness. "Thank you for the lovely dinner. Truly." She turned toward Mrs. Porter, who was still sitting on the stool in front of the piano, watching the two of them with a knowing expression, not fooled by their innocent words. "Thank you, Mrs. Porter. That was truly lovely."

"I was happy to play, and will do so at any time," she said as she pushed the stool out and dipped her head toward them. "Goodnight."

After she slipped out of the room, Levi placed his hand on Siena's lower back, guiding her toward the doorway. "It's getting late," he murmured in her ear, the growl returned, although this time, she welcomed it. "Thank you for the best night I believe I might have ever had."

"You are the one to thank. No one has ever done anything like this for me before," she said as they climbed the stairs together. "But I am not ready for the evening to be over."

"Are you not?"

"No," she said, and Levi thought it was overly endearing how she pressed her lips together to prevent the smile from emerging. "Perhaps we could extend the evening?"

"In what way do you suggest?" he asked, and with that she grabbed his hand and pulled him into her bedroom, shutting the door behind them.

"You made tonight so special for me," she said. "I would like to do the same for you."

He reached to take her in his arms, but she shook her head, trailing her fingers from his shoulders over his chest, her touch barely noticeable through the fabric of his jacket, waistcoat, and shirt.

Yet he could feel her deep within his soul.

"What are you doing?" he asked hoarsely, for he had a fair idea and yet he wondered how an innocent young woman such as she would have any idea that such a thing was even a possibility, let alone something she would be willing to try.

"I told you – I am doing something for you."

"But how—" he choked out.

"Eliza knows many things that a woman of her status should not," she said, looking up at him as her fingers reached his waistband. "She taught me a few things."

He knew that he should stop her, that this was not the sort of act he should allow a young woman like her to do, but when she began to unfasten the fall of his trousers, he found that he did not have the wherewithal to say no.

She gently tugged at the fabric, pulling the trousers down just enough to expose him. Her eyes widened slightly in surprise, but she didn't falter. Instead, she looked up at him with a shy smile before lowering her head.

Levi's breath hitched as her warm breath brushed against him. He tangled his fingers in her hair, the silky strands slipping through his fingers as she leaned closer. He could sense her hesitation, but there was also a determination in her movements that he found incredibly arousing.

She tentatively touched her tongue to him, and he cursed at the contact. She looked up at him, her brown eyes wide and uncertain. He nodded encouragingly, and she closed her eyes before taking him into her mouth.

Levi couldn't help the low groan that escaped his lips. She was so innocent, yet so eager to please him. Her lips were soft and warm around him, her tongue swirling gently, the sensation unlike anything he had ever experienced. He watched in awe as she slowly moved her head, her eyes closed, lost in the moment.

He could hear her breathing, shallow and quick, and he knew that she was as affected by the act as he was. He wanted to lose himself in her, to let go of his inhibitions and give himself over to her completely.

And she seemed eager to take him, to explore every inch of him, to make him feel completely and utterly alive. He would remember this moment for the rest of his life – the way she looked at him, the way she gently sucked and caressed him, the way she took him deep inside her mouth.

He never thought he would have this again — and not only a woman's touch but a touch that reached past his body to his heart.

The tension built within him, and he knew that he was close – so close – but he didn't want it to end.

She was still moving her head, her lips sliding up and down, her tongue darting out to touch him just so. Her eyes were closed tightly, her face flushed, her lips swollen and parted.

The tingling sensation spread throughout his entire body. He could feel it coming, the rush of pleasure threatening to overwhelm him.

But, as if she was unsure of what she was sensing, she pulled back slightly, gazing up at him with a mixture of concern and confusion.

"Are you well?" she whispered, her voice barely audible over the pounding of his pulse. "You're trembling."

He managed a soft nod, his eyes never leaving hers. "Just... a little shocked, that's all."

She nodded, her eyes widening slightly before she leaned forward once more, her lips closing around him again.

This time, he was ready. As she took him deep inside her mouth, his body convulsed, the pleasure building until he could take no more. With a loud cry, he thrust forward, his hips bucking uncontrollably as waves of pleasure coursed through him.

He kept his eyes closed as surrendered to the experience — to her — but then her hand gripped his hip, grounding him and bringing him back to reality. Her eyes were wide, her face flushed and her breath coming in short gasps. She looked up at him, her lips swollen and glistening, her eyes filled with a mixture of shock and triumph.

"Are...are you all right?" she asked breathlessly, her voice barely audible over the sound of their heavy breathing.

He had to laugh at that as he looked deep into her eyes. "I've never felt better in my life. You are an unbelievable woman, Siena."

Siena shook her head, her eyes still wide with disbelief. "I've never done...*this* before," she said, her voice barely above a whisper. "I was afraid I wouldn't be able to please you."

Levi cupped her face with both hands, his thumbs stroking her cheeks. "You do nothing *but* please me," he said. "And now it's my turn to do the same for you."

* * *

Before she could realize what was happening, he had reached down and picked her up, one arm under her knees, the other around her back as he walked her across the room and set her gently on the bed, tugging her forward until she was lying near the edge of it. He lifted her skirts, spreading them out around them, then knelt before her.

Just what was he about? Eliza had told her many things, but she had never told her about this.

He reached out and cupped her thighs, spreading her legs wider, then slowly began to lower his head. Siena gasped as his warm breath fanned over her most intimate place, and a delicate shiver ran through her body.

His tongue darted out, just the edge of it teasing the sensitive skin, and Siena felt a wriggle of desire unfurl deep inside her even as she was shocked beyond belief.

"Levi, is this—"

He lifted his head. "This is something I have been thinking about since you first walked into my life."

She had no answers for that, but knew she was safe with him, that he would never lead her astray.

Levi dipped his head, causing Siena to arch off the bed when he continued to explore, circling her folds with the flat of his tongue, drawing softly on the skin as he teased and tantalized.

Siena was lost in the pleasure, her breath catching in her

throat as she felt as if she were suspended on the edge of a precipice, waiting for the moment to push her over into the abyss of sensation. Levi's mouth was hot and wet, drawing her into the depths of his passion, and Siena felt as if she could never quite reach the bottom.

He continued to taste her, his lips and tongue worshipping her in a way that she would never have thought possible. Siena moaned softly as he suckled, her hips rocking against him in a rhythm that he matched perfectly. She felt as though she was being filled with fire, her body responding to his touch in the most exquisite of ways.

Levi pulled back for a moment, his gaze locked with hers as he looked up at her.

"Are you ready, Siena?" he whispered, his voice deep and husky.

Siena nodded, arching into him, and then, he touched that most vulnerable bud of nerves again and in moments, she unexpectedly tipped over the edge as her entire body began vibrating with the waves of heat and light that took her over.

She reached her arms out nearly frantically, needing Levi to anchor her, and soon they were filled with him as he pressed kisses softly over her cheeks, whispering in her ear.

"I've got you," he said. "I am here with you – how ever you need."

She nodded into his chest as he rolled her to her side, tucking her in next to his body. She knew that at some point, Mary would come to ready her for bed and Levi would have to leave her, but for now, she was content in staying exactly where she was – in his arms.

While the thought of leaving was becoming harder and harder to bear.

"I can see why you came here," she said softly. "This place... it's an escape from the rest of the world, a place where we can just be who we want to be, do what we want to do without worry about the repercussions or the judgements of others."

"It is that," he agreed, his breath warm on her ear, "but it can become far too comfortable as well. If I had never come upon you in the woods, then who knows what kind of man I would have turned into, alone without any company save for my servants, most of whom I had practically scared away from ever speaking to me."

"They are loyal to you," she said. "You are fortunate."

She could tell he was considering that for a moment. "I suppose you're right," he said. "I never would have considered myself a fortunate man after all that has happened to me, and yet…"

"Sometimes things come to us when we least expect it."

"On that," he said as he placed a kiss on the top of her head, "you are most certainly right."

"It is so strange," she said. "All of my life, my every moment was so closely controlled. I could never do a thing without the permission of one of my parents. This freedom to be able to act as I choose is a new, nearly overwhelming way to live. And now that I have it, I have no wish to be anywhere but with you."

He tugged her close and placed a kiss on the top of her head.

"I am not inclined to let you go anytime soon," he said, even though she could sense some melancholy in those words – as though the day would come when he would do so no matter his inclination.

It was a day that she had no desire for, but she would only stay if he wanted her.

She just wasn't sure how long she could wait for him to decide.

CHAPTER 17

*L*evi had breakfasted in his room for so long that he knew his staff was still becoming accustomed to serving him in the breakfast room.

But he would take any opportunity to see Siena.

She had not yet joined him, as she had likely slept late due to their activities last night. The thought produced a grin, although he was sure that she would be down shortly.

As Levi sipped his coffee and waited, Thornbury placed a paper down next to him, knowing that he enjoyed reading the news from London, even if he would never actually admit to it.

"The post arrived this morning, Your Grace," he said, to which Levi nodded absently, not taking much notice of it – until the headline at the top caught all of his attention.

Vanishing Virtue: Highborn Heiress Evaporates on Eve of Eminent Nuptials! Society in Uproar as Aristocratic Bride Disappears into Shadows of Intrigue!

The idea that there could be two missing brides within the nobility was certainly unlikely.

He picked up the paper, so intent on the story that he didn't notice anyone else enter the room.

> In a shocking turn of events that has sent the upper echelons of society into a frenzy, the beautiful Lady Siena Whitmore vanished on the day of her grand nuptials to the Baron Mulberry. Was it a daring escape or something much more sinister?
>
> Rumors abound of a clandestine affair with a mysterious suitor, a man deemed unsuitable by the rigid standards of high society. Could Lady Siena's heart have led her astray?
>
> Others suggest that the disappearance is shrouded in the dark veils of family intrigue. Could Lady Siena have unearthed long-buried secrets that propelled her to flee the impending union?
>
> Or was she ruthlessly snatched away from her true love just moments before they recited their vows to one another, and is now being held in a land far away against her will as she waits for her beloved to rescue her?
>
> The Baron Mulberry, left at the altar and bewildered by the sudden turn of events, has joined with Lord and Lady Sterling in issuing heartfelt pleas for the safe return of his intended bride. His grief and confusion have only

intensified the public's fascination with this captivating tale of love and loss.

As the search for Lady Siena ensues, society holds its collective breath, eager for the next chapter in this scandalous saga. Will the fair young lady return to the arms of the viscount, or has she truly forsaken her aristocratic destiny for the tantalizing allure of a love deemed taboo by the ton?

He cast the paper down in front of him, nearly chuckling at the amount of fiction within it.

Until he noticed Siena standing in front of him, her face white as she stared down at the table.

"What is this?" she asked, reaching out a shaking hand.

"It's nothing," he said, trying to hide it beneath the edge of the tablecloth. "Just an old scandal sheet. It's—"

"It's about me," she said, slowly sitting as she brought a hand to cover her mouth. "I suppose I should have expected that I could not just vanish without question, but I assumed – wrongly, obviously – that Eliza would see to an explanation." Her eyes flew up to meet his, and it didn't take her long to understand the grim expression he was wearing.

"No one will come here, Levi, I promise. No one knows I'm here. No one, except—" she hesitated, biting her lip.

"Eliza?" he finished, a brow raised.

"Yes, I did write her again, although I omitted nearly any mention of you besides this being one of your residences. There are also the tenants and the people from the village. I don't believe anyone saw me, but if they were talking to the servants, perhaps word of my presence here could have been shared that way. Unless you believe they will be loyal to you?"

He snorted. "Besides Thornbury and McGregor, I haven't exactly given my servants reason to be loyal. I showed up here and haven't spoken with any of the servants or tenants until the day the stables burned down."

"Oh," she said softly as she pushed the paper away from her as though it was offensive. "Well, I suppose all that I can hope now is that soon enough there will be another scandal, and everyone will forget about me."

"I highly doubt it," he scoffed. "You are a missing lady. A beautiful one of high birth. No one will ever forget you. If you do not appear again, your name will be remembered in the history books."

He stood now, unable to sit still any longer. "I should have thought of this before, but I didn't think you were staying here for any longer than it would take for the roads to clear. And then… well, then I became distracted. This is foolish, Siena. You cannot continue to hide here, pretending to all that you are what – dead? Lost? Gone forever?"

"I am not pretending anything," she said, standing as well and gripping the back of her chair, her knuckles turning as white as her face, causing a pang of regret to fill him, although he wasn't entirely sure what he was regretting – that he was saying these thoughts aloud? That he had formed this connection in the first place? "This is my life, Levi. I told you that this is the first time I can truly make choices for myself, so forgive me if it is taking longer than I had planned to determine what my next step might be."

"I'm sorry," he said, letting out a deep sigh, hating to see her like this, especially knowing that he was only adding to her discontent. "None of this is your fault, Siena. I take the blame. I told myself to enjoy this time with you without fear of the repercussions. Then the paper arrived this morning as a stark reminder that as much as I would like to think I live in my own world, disconnected from the larger one, it is still out there, with thoughts and opinions that do have substance, whether I like it or not."

Her gaze softened as she stared at him, before saying softly, "but does it truly matter? That is the world I ran from, and I have no intention of returning. What I have found here, with you, has had more meaning to it than anything that I left behind. Last night was magical, Levi, truly. Don't forget that man you were then."

"I am not forgetting him," he said, shaking his head. "However, I am also remembering the rest of the world."

"Can *I* not be your world?" she asked, the supplication on her face and in her voice melting the icy walls left around his heart.

He walked around the table toward her, taking her face in his hands. Her skin was so soft and impeccable, his scarred hand on her cheek in stark contrast. But then she nuzzled her face into it, and he was reminded that she had yet to show him any sign of caring about such a thing.

"I can see that becoming my reality, every single day that you are here," he said softly, and she closed the distance between them, pressing her lips against his.

It was a brazen act in the light of day, when any of the servants could step into the room and see them, but if she didn't care, then neither did he.

Which made him wonder when he saw the worry in her expression after she pulled away.

"I do have one concern," she said.

"Only one?" he asked lightly, although he was instantly filled with trepidation.

"There is speculation that I have been taken against my will or run away with a lover. Are you concerned that if I am discovered, you might be blamed?"

He hadn't considered that yet, which was foolish for it was a very valid concern, but he shrugged his shoulders.

"So be it. You will be there to disagree with them."

"Of course," she said, although she was obviously still troubled. "Although I would have to explain that I ran from my wedding, and if I am discovered…" she looked up at him with tears and worry swimming in her eyes, her next words on a whisper, "what if I am forced to return to him? To Lord Mulberry?"

He gripped her shoulders tightly. "I will never let that happen."

"How could you prevent it? My parents made an agreement with him. There was a dowry. I have no power to walk away. You might be a duke, but in this, you would be unable to stop them."

"If it came to that…" he said, closing his eyes as he gritted his teeth, not wanting to make her any promises but knowing he would do anything it took to prevent her from marrying another man, especially one like Mulberry, "then I would marry you myself."

* * *

Siena blinked at his words, trying to understand exactly what he was saying.

"Levi, did you just… propose marriage to me?" she asked.

"No," he said, holding up a finger between them. "I simply meant that if it came down to you having to marry Lord Mulberry, then I would marry you first."

"I see," she said as dejection filled her at his words. He didn't want her, not for the rest of their lives. When he had said he was living in the moment, he truly meant it.

"Siena, what are you thinking right now?" he asked, reaching out and taking her chin between his fingers.

She saw no reason not to be honest.

"I am thinking about the fact that you do not want me as I want you. That you do not feel the same emotions for me as I do for you."

He leaned forward, intent upon her.

"How much I want you and what I can offer you are two incredibly different things," he said. "Do not get them confused. The truth is, I want you very, very much, in every way possible."

"Then why—" she began, bewildered.

"Because the life I have to give you is not the one you deserve."

"Is that not up for me to decide?"

He stood back, crossing his arms over his chest for a moment as he remained silent, contemplative. "We shall see how long it is until you are finished with me and ready to return to the world you knew – or one better than it. I do promise you that while you are here, I will do all I can to keep you happy."

She regarded him, contemplating his words, wondering if there was more she could say, but eventually she simply nodded her head. "One day at a time."

* * *

As it happened, neither of them had to choose.

Later that afternoon, they were sitting in the library, each lost in their own book. Levi appreciated that with Siena, there was never a need to fill the quiet with mindless chatter, and yet he had a feeling that they were both uncertain of what to say, for neither of them were sure of just what direction to take next.

The butler interrupted them, his austere face wrinkled in consternation.

"Your Grace," he began before clearing his throat as though he was concerned about continuing.

"Yes, Thornbury?"

"It appears we have guests."

"Guests?" Levi repeated as he and Siena exchanged a glance. "Who?"

"I am actually not entirely sure. Collins spotted the carriage coming down the drive and thought it best to advise you before they arrived."

Levi moved purposefully to the front of the house, sensing Siena hurrying behind him trying to keep up. He knew he should slow but he couldn't seem to prevent his legs from their long, fast strides.

He stopped at the window of the drawing room so abruptly that Siena ran into the back of him.

The carriage, elegantly grand, clearly carried noble passengers. Its sleek black exterior was trimmed in gold with the family crest proudly displayed on the side among intricate designs. Levi struggled to recognize to whom it belonged, but it seemed that it wasn't here for him.

"Eliza!" Siena gasped, causing Levi to stiffen completely. He didn't follow Siena as she ran out past him in a flurry of cream skirts, leaving the drawing room for the front foyer. She didn't even wait for anyone to open the door for her, and it slammed heavily behind her as she ran out to embrace the richly dressed woman who disembarked from the carriage on his front drive.

So much for their interlude alone.

If there was anything he hadn't wanted, this was it. An intrusion on the peace he had finally found. He should have known.

Happiness was just not for him.

CHAPTER 18

"Eliza, it is so good to see you!" Siena said when her friend finally released her from her close grasp. "What are you doing here?"

"You told me you were here, so I came to rescue you," Eliza said, her arms still holding onto Siena's, looking her up and down as though to ensure that she was still whole and uninjured.

Siena could only laugh, for she had never felt safer.

"Rescue me? I do not need rescuing. I just wanted you to know I was healthy and well so you wouldn't worry. That was all."

"Well, I found I had no choice but to come make sure myself." She looked from one side to the other to make sure they were alone before she lowered her voice and dipped her head. "The Duke of Dunmore? Siena, what were you thinking?"

"I wasn't thinking anything. It is actually quite the story. Did you come alone?"

"No, of course not," Eliza said with a laugh. "Mother is

inside the carriage, still snoozing away. I hope you do not mind."

Siena shook her head, even as worry began to claw in her stomach. She enjoyed Eliza's mother, who was everything that Siena would have wished her own to be, and yet she had a feeling that Levi was not going to be thrilled about suddenly hosting an additional two guests.

Eliza leaned in and whispered, "what is he like?"

"The duke?"

"Of course the duke!"

"He is…" she began, uncertain of exactly how to describe him, but they were interrupted by the sound of hooves pounding against the gravel of the front drive.

They both turned around swiftly to see a figure pushing his horse, practically racing toward them, his dark cloak swirling behind him as though he were a prince come to rescue the fair maiden from the tower.

"I say…" Eliza said with a swift intake of breath. She had always been something of a romantic, as headstrong as she was.

"Well, well, who do we have here?" His voice was as gallant as the rest of him, the man swinging down from the horse in a rather fluid motion, although not quite as adeptly as Levi, in Siena's opinion.

"Is that Lord Fitzroy?"

It seemed that Eliza's mother had awoken, as she now stood on the stairs of the carriage, one hand in the footman's, who was helping her down.

The man gave an exaggerated bow toward her, circling his hand in the air as he did so.

"Lady Willoughby, how do you do? You are looking as lovely as ever."

Eliza's mother used her free hand to flutter her face. "You make an old woman blush, Lord Fitzroy. Next time I see your mother, I will have to tell her that she has raised far too great of a flirt. Now, Lady Siena, I know all too well what you are doing here after my daughter finally confessed to her antics, but Lord Fitzroy, I am rather confused about you."

"The Duke of Dunmore has always been a great friend of mine," he said. "I visit on occasion, for he is, fortunately, so close to London."

"That he is, thank heaven, for I am not particularly fond of long carriage rides," she said.

Siena and Eliza exchanged a glance, rather confused by the entire exchange from which they had been excluded.

"Lord Fitzroy, you do remember my daughter, Lady Eliza?" Lady Willoughby said once she finally reached them.

"Of course. I could never forget a beauty such as she," he said, bowing over Eliza's hand and kissing the back of it.

Siena noted with interest that Eliza's cheeks had grown a rather bright shade of red. Why, she had no idea, for Eliza was not one to be disconcerted by the presence of nearly anyone around her.

"And this is her dear friend, Lady Siena," she continued, and Siena bent in a low curtsy.

Lord Fitzroy's eyes rounded at that information. He was a handsome man indeed, with light brown hair that swept perfectly over his forehead once he had removed his hat, impish hazel eyes, and dimples that appeared in both cheeks when he smiled, which Siena guessed was quite often.

"The mysterious Lady Siena vanished right before her wedding," he said. "Are you aware that you are the talk of London? Everyone is wondering where you went, and if they have no information, they simply make it up. How astonishing to find you here."

"It is quite the story," Siena managed, noting with interest that she did not receive a kiss on the back of her hand. She stole a glance at Eliza, wondering if her friend had forgotten to tell her something about this Lord Fitzroy.

"Well, I must say that it is one that I am most eager to hear. But first, as lovely as it is to be in the company of such beautiful women, I cannot help but ask whether my good friend the Duke of Dunmore has met with some unfortunate demise, because I can see no other circumstance in which he would welcome company – besides mine, of course – on his doorstep."

He looked around at them expectantly, that smile still affixed to his face.

Siena opened and closed her mouth a couple of times, but she couldn't seem to find the right words to explain how this had all come to be.

But she didn't have to.

For it was then that Levi decided to make an appearance.

* * *

When Siena had rushed out of the house, ecstatic to meet her friend, Levi had remained exactly where he was, standing still and watching out the window.

He wanted to give Siena time with Lady Eliza.

He also had no wish to greet the woman himself, nor invite her into his home, although he couldn't exactly see a way around it at this point.

The truth was, he had no desire to welcome anyone save Siena, but he had known that to involve himself with her could have these repercussions. He just hadn't realized they would come so soon.

Then Fitz had come thundering up the drive and he had nearly groaned aloud.

The groan emerged when the second woman made an

appearance at the carriage door. A companion no doubt. Likely Lady Eliza's mother.

Just what he needed.

Levi ran his hand over his face, wondering if he closed his eyes and waited long enough they would all simply disappear like he was waking from a bad dream.

But no. When he opened his eyes, there they were, a band of people still standing on his front drive, bowing and curtsying to one another as though they were preparing to enter a ball of debutantes and not the lion's den.

Finally, he couldn't take the waiting any longer and he marched to the front door, wrenching it open to stare upon the lot of them.

They all stared back.

Siena with her usual tranquility, although her expression also held a wariness that he knew was due to worry over his response to Eliza's arrival.

Fitz with astonishment, which made sense for Levi would usually barely talk to even his oldest, most persistent friend.

And Eliza and her mother with the expressions of horror mixed with pity that he had come to expect from those seeing him for the first time. Or subsequent times, as it usually took people more than just one meeting to become used to his face.

"Your Grace."

The mother was the first to recover, likely from years of politeness both bred and trained into her. Her daughter followed suit, although while her horror either abated or she hid it well, a sense of curiosity remained as she studied him.

"Best come inside," Levi said, and when his stablehands and footmen quickly appeared, he wondered just how long they had been waiting, listening to see if he would welcome these visitors or turn them away.

"Truly?" Fitz said, and Levi could have throttled him. "You

want all of us inside? Please tell me we can at least use the drawing room and not all freeze in the study."

Levi nodded curtly as he told one of the footmen to stoke the fire in the grate. The man appeared confused, but a nod from Thornebury, standing in the doorway, sent him action.

Soon enough, they were all sitting awkwardly in the small, intimate, feminine drawing room.

Levi had taken one of the armchairs near the fireplace, Fitz the other. Siena, Lady Eliza, and Lady Willoughby were squished together onto the sofa.

Siena was fidgeting, her hands fisting her gown, and Levi longed to reach out and place his hands over hers to quiet them.

But he couldn't in front of an audience – for so many reasons.

"Thank you for having us," Lady Willoughby began, far too brightly.

"I never invited you," Levi replied, and Fitz leaned forward, likely to attempt to soften Levi's words, but there was no need. Levi had no intentions of making these people feel comfortable in his home.

"What His Grace meant to say was—" Fitz began, but before Levi could stop him, Siena jumped in, likely sensing Levi's discontent.

"H-how are my mother and father handling my disappearance?" she asked, to which Eliza and her mother exchanged a glance.

"They are concerned, of course," Lady Willoughby said, although her face belied something else altogether.

"Are they most concerned about breaking the commitment to Lord Mulberry, or about my welfare?" she asked, looking at Eliza, and Levi could sense the trust between them, although he wondered how galling the truth was going to be.

"The former," Eliza said, placing a hand on Siena's knee, likely to try to soften the blow. "You know you are too good for them."

Levi growled, causing the stares once more.

He couldn't help himself. Even though he knew such marriages were arranged more often than not, the thought of parents using a woman such as Lady Siena, so innocent, honest, and loyal, in such a manner, was nearly incomprehensible.

"Of course," Lady Willoughby interjected, "that still does not excuse this ruse my daughter put together for you to avoid the wedding, Lady Siena. To send you out travelling alone!" She shook her head. "If only Eliza had confided in me, then I would have made sure to send a few footmen with you."

Eliza and Siena both turned abruptly toward Lady Willoughby, mouths open in shock.

"You would have helped me?" Siena asked, blinking, and Lady Willoughby leaned in with a warm smile.

"You are not my daughter, Lady Siena, but if you hated this man so much to leave your entire life behind, then of course I would have helped. From where do you think my daughter received her daring nature?" Her eyes flicked over toward Levi before returning to Siena. "You must now tell me how you ended up here."

"It is quite the story," Siena said before starting in on her tale. Even though Levi had been there throughout most of her escapade, when she spoke of becoming lost and then the highwaymen discovering her, his heart hammered hard in his chest at the memory of her in such danger. He wasn't alone – they were all completely horrified.

Lady Eliza was biting her lip, a sheen of tears covering her eyes.

"Siena, I am so sorry," she said hoarsely. "This is all my

fault. I was so concerned about you leaving that I never stopped to consider the dangers that could befall you. The map should have taken you right to Streatham, but I could have made a mistake."

"This is not your fault at all, Eliza," Siena said. "I am a grown woman and can make my own decisions. I decided to leave, no matter the consequences. And while my journey was rife with danger, it led me here, where I have never felt safer."

Levi noted their incredulous stares, which he wasn't surprised about, although it seemed Siena couldn't quite understand it.

There was too much goodness within her.

He didn't deserve her – but for the first time, he was wondering if, perhaps, he might have to find it within himself to fight for her.

CHAPTER 19

Moisture had been gathering at the nape of Siena's neck as she sat in the drawing room with the gathered party.

She was surprised by her overwhelm from the scrutiny of both her closest friend and the man she was falling for. Siena could practically feel the curiosity radiating from Eliza as she sat beside her on the sofa, struggling to keep all of her questions inside until the two of them were alone.

Then there was Levi. The weight of his stare was heavy, and she could practically hear what he was thinking – that this was the reason he hadn't invited her in to stay with him, as her presence would invite others and their judgement.

The next time they had a moment alone, she would have to convince him that if there was anyone who would allow him to keep his peace and his secret, it was Eliza and her mother, who were nothing like what one would expect from most women of the *ton*.

But first, she must convince them of her safety.

"It is growing late," Lady Willoughby said once Siena had finished her story and they had all sat in some shock. "Your

Grace, I am so sorry to have intruded like this, but would it be far too forward of me to ask that we might be able to stay for the night, at least? We will have to decide on the next step forward for Siena, but first, I believe we could all use a good night's sleep."

"Of course," Levi said gruffly, although his tone made it clear that he was only agreeing because he had no other option. "I will speak to Mrs. Porter."

It appeared the housekeeper had already taken matters into her own hands, however, for she arrived at the door just as Levi was speaking to tell them all that the rooms were already prepared for their guests.

"Will Lord Fitzroy be staying?" she asked, and Siena had nearly forgotten Levi's friend as he sat beside him, his fingers steepled together as he watched and listened with interest.

"He'll be going," Levi said, just as Lord Fitzroy answered for himself. "Oh, I wouldn't miss this for the world," he said.

As Mrs. Porter hurried away, Levi growled, asking if he had the ability to make any decisions in this house that he owned.

Fitz only laughed, and Siena's heart warmed that Levi had a friend like him, who seemed to treat him no differently than he ever had before.

They agreed to reconvene at dinner, and Eliza grabbed Siena's hand as Mrs. Porter led them up the stairs and showed Eliza, her mother, and Lord Fitzroy to chambers on the opposite wing of Siena's bedroom. Siena followed her friend up the stairs, starting when she nearly ran into someone leaving the room.

"McGregor!" she said, pressing a hand against her breast. "You startled me. Us."

McGregor looked from Siena to Eliza and back again, his eyes narrowing slightly.

"The duke does not appreciate visitors."

Siena's eyes widened. "I know, McGregor," she said softly, appreciating his loyalty but knowing that Eliza wasn't pleased from the sharp intake of breath. "But Lady Eliza is my friend, and she will keep all of the secrets necessary. What are you doing in this chamber?"

"Delivering the bags."

"Oh, I thought the footmen would see to that," she said, confused.

"Just helping where I can. Good day, my lady."

Siena nodded, dismissing him, both ladies turning to watch him go.

"That was odd," Eliza said with a frown. "Is this what all of the servants are like?"

"No," Siena shook her head. "Most of them are quite lovely. McGregor was in the war with Levi, and I believe he has had a tough life. Levi has given him a chance to start over."

"The Duke of Death seems much more generous than most would think."

"He is," Siena said, trying not to bristle at the awful name that so many called him. "That's a moniker I believe should be forgotten."

"Of course. I apologize," Eliza said contritely as they entered the room. "I am glad we finally have a moment alone," Eliza said, sinking down on the bed. She paused for a moment to look around. "This room is very blue."

"Yes," Siena said with a slight laugh. "Every bedroom is a different color. Mine is as pink as yours is blue."

The décor of this room was all a rather faded blue, but at one point it likely had been a bright, vibrant royal hue. Now, the curtains appeared nearly striped from the difference the sun had made in parts of them, while the carpet in the middle of the room was worn, although the bed covering appeared to be newer than the rest of the room.

The windows looked out over the opposite side of the estate, providing a view of the sunset as it was dipping low over the horizon, causing a pink and orange brilliance to fill the sky.

"I understand that you said you feel safe, Siena, but you must tell me, has the duke been… respectful?"

Siena tried to hold back her reaction to her friend's question, but she couldn't help the giggle that rose up from deep within her. It began low in her stomach, and she covered her mouth with her hand to try to keep it inside, but it wasn't long until the laugh had bubbled out and Eliza's eyes widened in shock.

"I am not entirely sure what this means, but I have a feeling that I should be concerned," Eliza said, tilting her head, one of her dark curls bobbing off of her forehead. "*Should* I be worried, Siena? Oh goodness, what has happened? As much as I love seeing laughter within you again, you must stop that and tell me everything."

Siena's laughter finally abated, and she took pity on Eliza and came to sit next to her on the bed.

"When the duke first rescued me, I was frightened and untrusting of him, of course," she said. "But he opened his home to me, as much as he had no wish for visitors." She wasn't about to tell Eliza the entirety of Levi's story. He had told her that in confidence and she wouldn't break his trust. "Over time, however, I came to see another side of him. A side that is protective. That is compassionate. That loves with no bounds."

"Does he love you?" Eliza asked, leaning forward.

Siena sighed. "I am not entirely sure. I would like to think that he is on his way to loving me."

"My goodness, Siena," Eliza said, blinking. "This is quite the turn of events. I am… not judging you at all, as I feel you should do whatever makes you happy, but I wonder if your one act of rebellion has only urged you on to more."

Disappointment tugged her lips downward.

"I thought if anyone would understand, it would be you."

Eliza rushed forward. "I do, Siena, I do, I promise. Your heart is pure, and I know that you would never do anything out of spite or for scandal. I should know that better than anyone."

"Thank you," Siena said softly. "I do care for him. Truly."

"Are you going to marry him?"

"He would have to ask."

"Has he... compromised you?" Eliza whispered. "No judgement from me either way, but it might make a difference to your future."

"I wouldn't call it *compromising*," Siena said slowly, her cheeks now fiery as Eliza gasped. "But yes."

"Siena! Oh, you must tell me everything."

Siena couldn't help but laugh at that again.

"I do not think I could ever share such intimate details," she said. "But everything you ever taught me about a man and woman joining together was very helpful."

"Wonderful," Eliza beamed. "Although I must admit, that was all from research and not from experience, much to my dismay."

Siena snorted before becoming much more serious.

"I do not know what to say about the future. I do have tenderness for the duke, but I do not believe he wishes to ever marry, or welcome anyone to his home for an extended period of time. He wants to be alone. That is part of why he is here."

"Would you stay with him if he asked you to?" Eliza asked, and it took Siena a little longer to answer that.

"If he would have me and allow me the freedom to see you and do as I please, then yes."

"*If he would have you*? Why would he not? You are utterly perfect."

Siena could only shake her head at that, as she smiled somewhat regretfully.

"It is so much more complicated than that."

Eliza's blue eyes gazed intently into hers. "Any man – and I mean *any* man, duke or not – would be lucky to have you. You are the one who must find love, Siena, do you understand me?"

Siena laughed softly. "I understand."

"Do you miss London? Your family?"

Siena shook her head. "I miss you, of course, and a few of our other friends, but as sad as it is, I am glad to be gone from my family."

"They *are* rather horrid."

"Eliza!"

"Well, it's true, and if you won't say it, then I will say it for you." She sobered somewhat. "They are making a bit of noise about your disappearance. As is Lord Mulberry, although he is quick to retreat to his clubs, so no one is truly convinced of the suffering he claims."

"It will pass with the next scandal, will it not?"

Eliza shrugged. "I should hope so, but the rumors are increasing. They began by suggesting you ran away with a lover but now they are turning more sinister, saying that you were captured."

Siena nibbled her lower lip in worry. "If you are concerned that they will blame the duke if I am discovered, you should know that I have a similar fear, although he doesn't seem to share it. He says that if I am able to refute them, then nothing will come of it."

"One would hope. He *is* a duke – and yet, there is already so much speculation about him after the death of his brother."

"He is distraught about his brother's death," Siena said, swift to come to his defense. "Besides that, he has no wish to be a duke."

"You do not have to convince me," Eliza said, waving a hand. "It is the rest of the *ton*."

"Which is the very reason he hid here, away from the world," Siena mused. "Until I discovered him."

"Do not blame yourself for anything," Eliza said, "except for exploring the world as you have longed to and finding a man who sees you for the person you truly are. Now, we best get dressed for dinner. I know I didn't provide you much, so I managed to sneak a few dresses out of your house for you."

"You… snuck into my parents' house?" Siena said, following Eliza to the wardrobe as she pulled out familiar dresses and laid them in her arms.

"I did. I waited until I knew our parents were at an event together and then convinced a footman to accompany me and sneak in. Even my mother wouldn't have approved."

Ignoring the fact that her parents had gone to a social event despite a missing daughter, Siena could hardly believe what Eliza was saying.

"What if you had been caught?"

Eliza laughed. "That is far from the most daring escapade I have undertaken."

"Well, thank you," Siena said, somewhat bewildered by her friend, although she always had been.

"Did you like the lilac gown I packed you? It was one of my favorites."

"I did love it. But… it is destroyed."

That had Eliza stopping what she was doing and turning around to face her in shock. "Destroyed? How?"

Siena sighed. "It is another long story, but one that includes a fire in the stables."

"Recently?"

"Yes."

"My goodness, Siena, but this man has bad luck with fires. Do you think that, perhaps, there just might be something to the rumors—"

"No," Siena said swiftly. "Absolutely not."

Eliza nodded, although she didn't appear convinced. "Very well. If you say so. It just seems like quite a coincidence for one man to be struck by multiple fires, does it not?"

"I don't know, Eliza," Siena said softly. "I agree that there must be more to it, but I have no answers for you other than knowing that the duke had nothing to do with it."

"If you believe it, then I do too," Eliza said confidently.

"You are a good friend, Eliza."

"There is none better than you."

They shared a smile.

"Now," Siena said, narrowing her eyes at her, "you must tell me about Lord Fitzroy."

"Lord Fitzroy?" Eliza said, her eyes widening, although her innocence seemed somewhat feigned. "There is nothing to tell."

"Are you sure about that? When you saw him, you seemed rather… overcome."

"Not at all," Eliza said, tossing her hair back behind her. "Our families are friends of course. That is all."

"But you would tell me if there was something there?"

"Of course," Eliza said, a smile covering her face, although Siena had the feeling that it was rather forced. "You would be the first to know."

CHAPTER 20

Levi would have preferred to be many places other than this dinner.

But at least Siena was here. Her presence made everything he typically avoided far more bearable. Anytime he wished to escape, or caught someone scrutinizing his scars, he would look at her and calm would return.

Fitz, at least, provided entertainment for the rest of them. He could spin a story like no one else, and he had the ladies hanging onto his every word. Levi couldn't help the jealousy that Siena was one such woman, but then, it was not as though *he* had any intention of regaling them into laughter, now was it?

Fortunately, dinner came to a close sooner rather than later, his staff overly eager to serve a house party, although Levi's hopes for a reprieve from the ladies and time alone with Fitz were dashed when Lady Willoughby suggested that they all retire to the drawing room together.

He was about to decline when Fitz stepped in and enthusiastically agreed, suggesting they play a few games of cards.

Before they had a chance to begin, however, Lady Eliza

surprised Levi by appearing by his side and asking for a moment of his time. He paused, about to say no, but then he caught Siena's eye from across the room. Her pink lips curled up into a small smile, and he could feel the affection shining out of her eyes toward him.

It was at that moment, he realized, that he would do absolutely anything for her.

"Very well," he murmured, following Lady Eliza as she began a turn about the room. Levi recalled these courting rituals well, although he hadn't missed them when he had left London.

"I appreciate you rescuing Siena in her time of need," she said, and Levi had a sense that Lady Eliza was a woman who always came straight to her point, which he appreciated.

"There is nothing to thank me for."

"There is, as I was the one who sent her away alone. It was foolish of me, I will admit, but I was only thinking of helping her escape from Lord Mulberry. I should have planned to accompany her, at least, or arranged for a travelling companion. I just had no idea until the very last moment that she would actually leave."

"Lady Siena is a grown woman, Lady Eliza. She can make her own choices."

"That she can," Lady Eliza agreed. "Which brings me to my reason to speak to you. Siena has told me that the two of you share… feelings for one another, let's say. I need to know if they are as true for you as they are for her. I do not want to see her heartbroken and as much as it seems as though you are a good man at heart, I cannot help but worry that you might not be able to provide her what she needs."

Her words almost caused him to come to a stop, and he rubbed a hand over his brow, where his scar often itched him.

"If you are questioning my feelings for her, then you have nothing to worry about. They are as true as can be."

"I sense a 'however.'"

He gave a humorless chuckle. "You would be right. *However*, feelings alone don't matter. I also have to think about what kind of life I can offer her, what it would be like for her to continue to live here, with me, shut away from the rest of the world."

"You do not *have* to be shut away."

"That is easy for you to say, Lady Eliza, when you are not seen as a murderous beast by the *ton*."

"Perhaps not, but it is not as though I am, exactly, a diamond of the first water. I am spoken about as well, although perhaps not for my appearance."

He shook his head, sighing out his frustration. "I would never break her heart. But I worry that one day she would wake up and wonder what she is doing with me."

"Were you not the one who just told me that she is a grown woman who can make her own decisions?"

He couldn't help his snort. "You are quick witted, Lady Eliza, I will give you that. I just do not understand how she can bear to look at me day in and day out and not be confronted with the monster that I am."

Eliza was silent for a moment, clearly considering her words, before she stopped and looked him straight in the eye, her voice hushed as they remained on the other side of the room, just out of hearing of the rest of their party.

"Siena has the purest heart out of anyone I have ever met, and I am not just saying that because she is my closest friend." She leaned forward, conviction in her every word. "If there is good within you, she will find it. Her love is not a gift to be taken advantage of, nor to be wasted. Do you understand me?"

Her nostrils flared slightly with her obvious protective spirit.

"I do," he said, understanding. "I can promise you one thing."

"Yes?"

"Anything I do for her will be done with her very best interests at heart."

She scrutinized him for a moment before nodding. "Very well. I suppose I can accept that." She paused before looking up at him, her gaze softening somewhat, not with pity but rather with an understanding that he hadn't expected from so forward a woman.

"I am sorry for all that you have been through, Your Grace. I cannot imagine how hard it must have been to lose your family and be injured yourself."

"Thank you, Lady Eliza," he said, appreciating her words more than he'd like to admit.

She turned around and returned to the women, leaving Levi to shake his head after her. Lady Eliza was clearly a good friend, that much was for certain.

Fitz sent him a look of question, but he just shrugged, for there was nothing to say.

Siena was too good for him, yes, but she was too good for any man.

Now he just had to decide what exactly he was going to do about it.

* * *

Siena couldn't sleep that night.

She tossed and turned, too caught up in visions of what her future could or could not look like floating around in her mind.

She was becoming more aware that what she wanted was

right in front of her, in the form of a man. One she had never seen coming, the type of man she had never considered.

Levi.

He had seemed uncomfortable tonight, yes, but he had been there. He had made conversation when required, had even quirked a smile now and then when Lord Fitzroy cracked one of his jokes. She had no hopes of him returning to polite society, but then, neither did she have much interest in society doing so.

The thought of a reappearance in London or even an event including more guests than those here with her actually caused her discomfort as well. If she was discovered, what would happen to her? She had escaped her wedding, but at what expense?

Finally, she decided that there was only one way she was going to find any sleep.

She pushed open her door before tiptoeing down the corridor and lightly knocking on Levi's door.

She left her room, wondering if she was, perhaps, being foolish. He could be asleep or wishing for time alone after the company that he'd had to keep that night, all because of her.

When the door creaked open, the sound echoing throughout the quiet house, all of her worries evaporated.

The light from the moon through the windows behind him cast a soft glow on Levi's silhouette. His hair was tousled, sticking out in all directions, his shirt and trousers were wrinkled and rumpled, likely having just been pulled on to open the door, his chest peeking out through the buttons of his shirt.

He looked her up and down with a slight smirk on his face as he adjusted his eyepatch.

"Well, if it isn't the little rebel," he growled out.

She laughed lightly. "I couldn't sleep, and I thought – well, I wanted to see you."

He held open the door. "Come in," he said. "At this point we are past inviting scandal."

"We are fortunate that everyone else is sleeping on the other side of the house."

Levi snorted. "I believe that has less to do with fortune and more to do with my staff, who are far more interfering than they should be."

"They are looking out for your best interests," she said.

"Which I appreciate now," he said, reaching an arm out toward her. "Come."

She went willingly, eagerly, sitting on his lap with her arms wrapped around his neck. She leaned in, tilting her head up. He accepted her invitation, capturing her lips in a searing kiss. The world around Siena faded away as she lost herself in the sensation of Levi's lips on hers, his touch stirring deep-rooted feelings.

Levi's hands moved to her waist, pulling her closer as he deepened the kiss. Siena's heart raced as she realized that this man had, so unexpectedly, captured her heart.

As their lips parted, they gazed into each other's eyes, both breathing heavily. Raw emotion reflected in Levi's gaze, a vulnerability that touched her soul and made her feel truly seen for the first time in her life.

"I never expected to find someone like you," Levi whispered, his voice husky with emotion. "Even before everything changed in my life, I didn't truly believe that a woman for me existed."

"Perhaps there wasn't at that time," she said. "Perhaps I am only right for the man you are now, and not the man you were then."

Levi's hands traveled up her back, tangling in her hair as he pulled her closer, kissing her deeply once more.

His thumb brushed gently against her cheek, wiping away a stray tear. "I want to spend the rest of my life getting to know every inch of you, Siena," he said, his voice filled with raw emotion, his eye gazing into hers.

"You want to," she whispered, "but will you?"

He didn't answer her then, instead leading her over to the bed, where he provided her with no more words but instead worshipped her body, peppering kisses over her skin, discovering every curve and dip that made her body uniquely hers. Siena felt a sense of liberation, of being truly alive as Levi's hands explored her with reverence and desire.

He didn't draw anything out this time, slowly notching himself inside of her and moving in and out, finding a rhythm that was as old as time, each touch igniting a fire — one that they both allowed to consume them. Siena released all of her inhibitions, giving herself completely to the man who had unexpectedly stolen her heart, and soon enough they were coming together, overwhelmed by both their pleasure as well as the emotion that this night had revealed.

As the night turned into dawn, they lay entwined in each other's arms, the light of a new day peeking through the curtains. Siena traced lazy patterns on Levi's chest, his heart beating steady beneath her touch.

"I could stay here forever," Levi murmured, pressing a kiss to the top of her head.

Siena lifted her gaze to meet his. "As could I," she replied softly. "But reality will soon come knocking at our door – likely in the form of your valet."

Levi's expression darkened slightly at the reminder of the world they would, at some point, have to face.

But not right now.

Right now, they would simply enjoy one another.

CHAPTER 21

Levi couldn't stop smiling the entire next morning.

As much as it was possible for him to actually smile.

It wasn't only because he had spent the night with Siena. It was that she had sought him out. She had needed him. He couldn't remember the last time someone had needed him, and not just for what he could provide but for who he was.

He still avoided his little makeshift house party – the one that he had no desire to be hosting – but he found himself seeking Siena out that afternoon, eager for time alone with her.

He discovered her in the front parlor with Lady Eliza and Lady Willoughby, looking out over the front drive beyond them as they took tea together.

"My apologies for the interruption," he said gruffly, not enjoying the way they were all staring at him, although rationally he understood that he was the one speaking, standing in the doorway as he was, although as far from their scrutiny as possible. "Lady Siena, I was wondering if you might join me for a walk in the gardens?"

The beam that lit her face was worth his discomfort. "I would love to," she said. "That is, Lady Willoughby and Eliza, if you do not mind."

"Of course not, dear," Lady Willoughby said, patting her hand. "We shall see you afterward. Enjoy yourself."

Siena collected her hat before joining him, smiling up at Levi and slipping her arm through his as they stepped out into the sunshine. When she closed her eyes and lifted her head to the sky, he realized that it wasn't the sun that was warming him. It was her.

She was changing something within him, lifting the weight that had been sitting on his shoulders for far too long.

He was so caught up in her that he didn't notice the commotion far up the drive until it was too late.

Siena's head snapped forward at the noise of the horse's hooves against the gravel, and she stiffened as she turned and looked up at him frantically.

"Levi," she said, "who is that?"

The alarm in her voice mirrored his own unease, but her fear was much more justified than his own discomfort. If these new visitors were here for her, then it could mean that everything she had worked so hard to overcome could come crashing down around her, sending her right back to the prison she had escaped.

He could not allow that to happen.

"I do not recognize them," he said, lifting a hand to shield his eyes to try to make them out, having to fight all that was within him to stop himself from turning around and running backward into the house. "They are all on horseback."

"There are three of them," she noted, and then gasped, her panic a squeeze around his heart.

"What is it?"

"The man in front… is my father."

Levi wrapped his arm around her protectively, holding

her close against him, wishing that he could hide her away to keep her safe and away from any harm.

But it was too late for that.

The arrival of these men was a reminder of one thing he'd had no choice but to learn – there was no hiding. For eventually, all truth came to light, and it was better to face it head on and address it rather than live in fear.

Levi had tried to fight before – for the life of his brother, for everything that he had held dear. He had failed then, and he vowed that he would do everything he could to be strong for Siena, to keep her safe from the harm that threatened, even if it was from her own family.

"I cannot go back, Levi," she said, her voice just above a whisper. "Please, don't let me go back."

"I won't," he vowed, keeping her tucked into his side while they walked together to meet her father at the front of the drive. He wished that instead of just enjoying his time with her and forgetting all that could threaten, that he had done this the right way and had made her his wife in reality and not just in his dreams.

"There he is!" came the cry of her father, his arm outstretched toward the two of them as the men thundered up the drive. "Unhand my daughter!"

He rode stiffly, almost fighting his horse, his chin raised, exuding an air of superiority. His thin lips were pinched together, his gaze accusatory. Levi instantly hated him.

He came to a stop in front of them, and Levi took the moment to stand on the bottom stair and tower above him, showing him that he was not afraid and would not back down.

The men behind Lord Sterling appeared less confident, and Levi reminded himself that no matter what else was true, his title was higher than any of those before him could be.

"You," Siena's father said as he climbed the stairs toward

the two of them. "You... *beast*. Killing your own brother wasn't enough? You also had to kidnap my daughter?"

"Father, he did no such thing," Siena said, trying to step in front of Levi, but he held her back. He wasn't going to have her put herself in any danger, and he was certainly going to make sure that she stayed safe.

"I would never kidnap a woman," Levi said, his voice low and steely, hoping that this man would understand that he was not a man to cross. "Nor would I ever take the life of anyone in my family."

"No?" Lord Sterling sneered. "I have heard many things about you. The Duke of Death, they call you."

"I did my duty in war," Levi returned. "That has no bearing on my life now that I have returned."

"You should be thanking him, Father," Siena intervened. "Not only did he fight for our country, but he fought for *me*. If it wasn't for him—"

"Then you would be married to Lord Mulberry right now, where you belong," her father finished.

"I most certainly do not!" Siena exclaimed, and as much as he hated this entire situation, Levi was proud of her for voicing her opinion, for standing up for herself.

"I will see you tried, and I will see you hanged," Lord Sterling said, pointing a finger in Levi's face. "The magistrate has accompanied me to see that all is returned as it should be and that you face the consequences you deserve. Grant, take him into custody."

Levi reached up and wrapped his hand around Lord Sterling's finger, squeezing it as he pushed it down between them.

"Show some respect," Levi said, before turning to challenge the magistrate. "Well?"

The rather portly man stood behind Sterling, shifting

from one foot to the other nervously. "My lord, you never told me the man in question was a duke."

"He kidnapped my daughter!"

"Perhaps, but he is a *duke*. This is not a case for me. This is for the House of Lords."

"But until then—"

The magistrate was shaking his head. "You will have to take this to them, my lord. There is nothing I can do."

Lord Sterling was so upset he was practically shaking in anger, but he finally bit out, "Fine. I will do just that. And once this goes through the other lords who learn the story, then I'm sure they will see what must be done. You know the rumors about you, *Your Grace*. They will know the truth about what has happened here."

"You have no idea of the truth," Levi said.

"Siena, the carriage is just a short distance behind us as we rode ahead," her father said. "When it arrives, we will return to London. Lord Mulberry is waiting. I'm sure we can explain all of this away. When you return from this ordeal that you have faced after being snatched away from your wedding, we will make sure you are seen as the darling of London, that you had no participation in this and that you were only waiting to be rescued."

"Absolutely not," Siena said, crossing her arms over her chest and leaning into Levi. "I will not marry that man."

"You will," her father said, leaning in toward her. "You have no choice. The dowry — a significant one —has been paid and he is waiting for his rights as a husband. His rights meaning you. He has threatened to bring a breach of promise lawsuit upon us."

"While he wanders about London nightclubs and finds other 'rights'?" she returned, which only caused her father to glower in anger. If there wasn't an audience, Levi had no doubt that Sterling would have struck her right then.

"A man can do as he wishes. Now—"

"Lord Sterling, what do you think you are doing?"

Lady Willoughby appeared in the doorway behind them, and as much as Levi had regretted her arrival, he now had a change of heart, most thankful that she was here to provide a buffer between Lord Sterling and him and Siena.

"Lady Willoughby, what in the hell are you doing here?"

"That's no way to speak to a lady," Levi growled, causing Lady Willoughby to look at him in surprise. In truth, he was sure that she had heard far worse in her life, but he would take any opportunity to oppose Lord Sterling.

"Thank you, Your Grace," she said with a nod in Levi's direction. "Now, perhaps we should move this conversation inside? This is all rather untoward, standing on the front step and shouting at one another. You should know better, Lord Sterling."

She turned around and continued into the house, not accepting any argument. Siena looked up at Levi, a touch of hope lighting her face.

"I will be going, then," the magistrate said, backing his horse away. "Sorry to have disturbed you, Your Grace."

He rode off while Collins appeared behind them, looking to Levi for guidance as to whether he should see to the other two horses.

Levi nodded, figuring that the men were going to be here for a time, then he followed the rest of them into the house. As they made for the drawing room, he couldn't help but consider how much he had grown to hate this room, which had become the place where he was hosting all of his uninvited guests.

"Well," said Lord Fitzroy, who stood in the doorway. "This is a most unfortunate surprise. Lord Hanson," he said in greeting, identifying the second man who must have been a colleague of Lord Sterling's. Levi didn't altogether care as long as they left his house as quickly as they had appeared – without Siena.

Lord Sterling had seemed to calm somewhat with the appearance of Lady Willoughby, although he was still tapping his foot on the floor impatiently.

Siena and Levi sat together on the sofa, a united front against her father.

"How did you know I was here?" Siena asked once they sat, and her father scowled.

"Servants. Isn't that how we always learn everything?"

Levi inwardly sighed. He had hoped he could trust everyone in his staff, but obviously there was someone who wasn't as trustworthy as he would have liked.

"I came as soon as I learned that you were with this… man," her father said, nearly shivering in disgust. "I wasn't sure if I would find you alive or not."

"Did you really care about my health, or were you more concerned about whether or not you could return me to Lord Mulberry?" she asked, tilting her head, studying him as she awaited his answer.

"Does it matter?"

"I suppose not," she said, sadness in her voice, "although I wish it was the former. Be that as it may, all you need to know, Father, is that His Grace saved me from a disastrous fate when I was accosted by highwaymen. He has been most accommodating to me and to Eliza and Lady Willoughby. You can see there is no scandal as I have a chaperone."

"But there is scandal," Levi said, surprising even himself. As Siena had spoken, he had seen only one solution. One that, he must admit, he was actually happier to offer than he would have guessed. "Siena will not marry Lord Mulberry."

"Why the hell not?" Lord Sterling burst out.

"Because she is going to marry me instead."

CHAPTER 22

The room was silent for only a moment, stunned into silence, until Lord Fitzroy pushed himself off of the wall and called out, "Congratulations!"

Eliza was the next to offer her excitement, stepping over and wrapping Siena in a hug. "Are you sure?" she whispered in her ear, to which Siena could only nod, so overwhelmed was she by these sudden turns of events.

"You most certainly are not!" Lord Sterling burst out. "I will not have my daughter married to a—to a—"

"To a duke?" Lady Willoughby supplied, arching an eyebrow and causing Lord Sterling to curse.

"It is too late. You have a marriage contract with Lord Mulberry. To break it would be of great offense."

Siena stood, staring her father in the eye. She was done with this, with being told what to do, being used as a pawn in these games between men.

"I love Levi, and if he will have me, then I will marry him," she said, lifting her chin. "You cannot tell me what to do any longer."

Lord Sterling began to chuckle lowly, in such a sinister manner that terror began to creep down Siena's spine.

"You think you know everything, but you have no say in this, Siena," he said. "You will see."

With that, he turned and left the room, Lord Hanson following behind him sheepishly. Siena and Eliza exchanged a look, both of them knowing her father far too well to trust that he was done with them.

Siena could tell that Levi's silence was an uncomfortable one, and she took a step toward him, placing a hand on his. "Levi, are you all right?" she asked, to which he gave a terse nod and said, "Fine," although he most certainly was not.

She tugged on his hand, leading him away from the others. Eliza and her mother were murmuring in low voices to one another while Lord Fitzroy watched them all with concern on his normally smiling face.

"I'm so sorry, Levi," she said hoarsely. "The last thing you wanted was company or attention and I have brought both upon you. I feel that all I have done since I arrived is place a burden upon you. Yes, there have been good moments, but overall—"

Despite the others in the room, Levi leaned forward and cupped her cheeks in his hands.

"The good moments kept me going through any trying ones," he said. "I will do anything for you, Siena. Whatever you need."

Siena realized belatedly that she had just announced to everyone that she loved him. He had agreed to marry her, but he had yet to tell her how he felt about her in return. Would he think her foolish for saying so? Did he feel the same?

"Are you sure about this?" she asked. "About m-marriage? If you aren't, I understand. We – *I* will find another way. Eliza and Lady Willoughby will help as well. The last thing I want to do is to subject you to a life that you have no wish for."

He looked away from her for a moment, and she knew then that he had doubts.

"Tell me how you truly feel," she implored. "Now, before it is too late."

"Do I have concerns?" he said, his brow furrowing. "Of course I do. If we have children, are they going to fear me? Will you be able to live the life that you deserve, a life full of love, light, and people? I'm not sure that I will ever be able to give you that."

He took a ragged breath as Siena tried to calm her pulse, which had begun to beat quickly at Levi's mention of children. "If your other option was someone worthy of you, I would tell you to go to him. But I will not have you return to the life you left, nor a man like Lord Mulberry."

"So…" she took a breath, trying not to allow him to see how affected she was, "you would marry me only to protect me?"

His hands rose again to cup her face, as he stared at her intently, as though wishing that he could tell her exactly what he was thinking without actually saying anything. "Siena—"

"I hate to break up this moment," Eliza said, her voice cutting through the circle of calm that had surrounded Siena, "but just where do you think your father went? It isn't like him to leave without the last word. What do you think he will do now?"

"I hate to think of it," Siena said, biting her lip, before looking up at Levi, wondering what he had been about to say to her, wishing Eliza hadn't interrupted them.

"He will try to coerce you to return to London with him, I would suspect," Lady Willoughby said, walking over to join them. "As much as it pains me to say this, he has a point. Your

Grace might rank above him, but when it comes to you, Siena, you might have little recourse if your father has already agreed with Lord Mulberry."

Her eyes flicked over to Levi.

"There is one man who would be able to prevent him from doing as he wished with her — her husband."

Levi smiled grimly. "Well. How fortunate that we are so close to Canterbury."

Lady Willoughby's eyes lit with glee, confusing Siena.

"Canterbury?" Siena repeated. "What does that have to do with anything?"

Lord Fitzroy pushed himself off the wall. "Canterbury, my dear, is the home of the *Archbishop* of Canterbury. The one man in England who could grant you a special license to marry whenever and wherever you wish."

Levi's eyes met Lord Fitzroy's. "Could you go in my stead? I wouldn't like to leave Siena."

"Say no more," Lord Fitzroy said with a bow. "On my way out, I will ask Thornbury to send a footman for the vicar."

"What is happening?" Siena said, turning around in Levi's arms, looking up at him in bewilderment.

"We are getting married," he said, although he did not look at all like a man who was in the throes of love, about to take his bride. "Fitz will go seek a special license from the Archbishop, and in the meantime we will prepare so that we can marry as soon as he returns. Then your father will no longer be able to take you away. I suspect he has returned to London to gather forces to come and ensure that you have no choice but to go with him. We must be faster."

Siena froze at his words, captured both by a sense of how unfair it was that she had to endure this and buoyed by hope that there was an escape from her predicament – but at what cost?

"Are you sure, Levi?" she asked, her voice just above a whisper. "I know you wanted nothing to do with this and here I am—"

"I would not have offered if I didn't mean it," he said, more gently now. "Why don't you and Lady Eliza go prepare for the wedding? I know it is likely not the wedding day that you envisioned, but perhaps you can make it bearable."

She nodded woodenly as Eliza threaded her arm through hers and led her out of the room. They were already upstairs and walking down the corridor when the severity of all that was happening hit her.

"Eliza," she said, stopping and staring at her friend. "I do not know if I can do this. It is all so sudden, and I am not sure if Levi actually has any wish to marry me or if he is doing it out of some strange sense of honor. He never wanted to be married, never even wanted anyone at his estate. What if we marry and then he grows to resent me and his life if this was just an act of duty, a lesser evil of the two choices? He had made a vow to protect me, but is ensuring that I do not return to Lord Mulberry worth sacrificing his wishes? Oh goodness, this has been one pre-wedding panic too many."

She finally stopped when Eliza wrapped her hands around her upper arms and stared at her intently.

"Siena, take a breath," she ordered. "You are overthinking this."

"Overthinking?"

"Yes. You are looking for faults when they are not there. The entire situation is not ideal, true, but I do believe the duke loves you – or, at the very least, cares for you deeply. He may say that he does not want this life, but maybe he is wrong. Maybe you have to *show* him what he wants and help him to understand that he is worthy of it."

"But—"

"He does not strike me as the kind of man who would do

something he had no wish to do," Eliza said, and Siena nodded slowly, thinking back to the many times he had declined her suggestions. "In the very worst outcome, if you both truly decide that you have no desire to live together, then you can return to London — hopefully with the children you have always longed for —and live the life you choose while he remains here or wherever he will be. But at least your father will no longer have authority over you."

Siena swallowed hard. "I think that would be even sadder than not being married to him at all," she said hoarsely. "To know that he truly didn't want me, despite me being his wife."

Eliza smiled sympathetically. "I know, Siena. I do. Those are all valid concerns, and I know that you will solve them in time. But right now, in this moment, it is most important that you prevent being forced to return to Lord Mulberry."

"I love him," she said, her voice wavering now. "Levi, that is, although he has never said the same."

"Perhaps he doesn't know how he feels," Eliza said. "There is a good chance that he just hasn't yet realized that he needs you just as much – if not more – than you need him."

Siena brightened somewhat at the thought as Eliza continued.

"Perhaps it is up to you to show him that he is worthy of love, that there is more to him than what he looks like or the sum of his experiences. Has he changed since you arrived?"

"Most incredibly," Siena whispered. "But it is not that he is a different person. He has found who he truly is."

"With a bit more time together, you might be surprised at the life the two of you are able to create for yourselves."

"That could be," Siena said with a watery smile. She wanted to believe Eliza, truly she did, but it seemed as if the entire world was against them at the moment.

"He is fighting for you," Eliza said, giving her arms one

last squeeze before standing and walking over to the wardrobe, opening it and placing her hands on her hips. "Now. What are you going to wear for your wedding day?"

CHAPTER 23

itz, thankfully, arrived back from Canterbury before Lord Sterling returned. He rode up the drive with a huge grin on his face, and even though his friend had successfully completed a great favor for him, Levi couldn't help grunting, "Took you long enough."

Fitz, of course, was not affected by his surly mood as he simply grinned even wider and planted the license in his hand. "Is the vicar here?"

"He is."

"Where is your bride?"

Fitz looked around the foyer as though expecting her to appear, but Levi hadn't seen her since she had gone to her chamber with Lady Eliza.

"Coming soon," he said instead, even though a large part of him was worried that she might not appear. She had run away from a wedding once before. What was stopping her now? Lady Eliza, the escape artist, was here with her. What if she convinced Siena to run away again, this time to follow through on her plan to meet this friend of hers or to run even farther?

He didn't want to think of it. For the first time, he was actually considering what his future might look like, and there was no other option than to have Siena in it. He'd had a taste of her love and now he wasn't sure that he could live without it any longer.

He heard a noise on the landing above him and he turned to see Siena walking along the railing, Lady Eliza at her side. He released a long breath that he hadn't even realized he had been holding.

"There she is," Fitz said, clapping his hands together, but Levi didn't say anything, for he couldn't take his eyes off her.

She wasn't wearing anything extravagant. It was a dress he had seen her in before, a light rose muslin, and yet with the blush in her cheeks, the glimmering of the chandelier off of her hair and the way her brown eyes stared at him with trepidation yet trust, she was more beautiful than anyone he had ever seen.

A nudge pushed him forward slightly, and he turned to find Fitz waving him on, which finally sprang him into action as he walked over to the bottom of the landing and held his arm out to her.

"Siena," he murmured, and a smile touched her lips as she placed her hand on his arm.

She looked up at him, worry in her expression. "Are you sure about this?" she said. "If you are not, we can find another way. I promise."

He knew he hadn't exactly asked in the way he should have, so caught up he had been in ensuring her safety, but now he took both of his hands in hers, forgetting Fitz, Lady Eliza, that anyone was threatening them as he brought them close to his chest and leaned in so that they were sharing the air between them.

"I want nothing more than to be married to you," he said in a low voice. "I know that there might be obstacles along the way, but I have never been happier than when I am with you. I promise I shall be as good of a husband as I can be. That might not mean much, but it is all I am capable of. If that is enough for you, then of course I will marry you."

"That is more than enough," she said, a sheen of tears covering her eyes, and he leaned in and kissed her nose, wishing he could rid her of all of her sadness. "We will find a way forward; however you choose."

He nodded, uncertain exactly of what he should say at the moment, but one thing he knew – of any woman in the world, he would choose her. Again and again.

"Well, then," he said with what he hoped was an encouraging smile, "are you ready to become a duchess?"

"Oh, goodness," she said, appearing so shocked that he nearly laughed. "I hadn't even considered the duchess part."

"Not to worry, I do not take the role of duke too seriously," he said, beginning to lead her back to the drawing room.

"You should," she insisted. "The dukedom plays an important role to a great many people."

Levi had no wish to have this conversation at the moment, but he was glad, at least, that it had distracted her from her worry over what was to come.

He still wasn't certain if he was doing the right thing. The right thing probably would have been to find another place for her, to help her escape and find the life that she wanted to live. But selfishly, he couldn't let her go. He wasn't sure if he loved her. He had never truly felt love before, so how could he know? But he did know that he had a fierce need to protect her, a need that overcame all other emotion, and he couldn't trust anyone but himself to properly look after her.

So, marry her he would.

As they stepped into the drawing room, Lady Eliza pressed a bouquet of freshly cut roses into Siena's arms. Siena's mouth parted in surprise. Levi had asked Thornbury to make sure that they were prepared for her. Another sat in a vase near the front of the hearth, which had become a makeshift altar of sorts. The fire burned low in the grate, although far enough away from them that it wouldn't distract him.

With Lady Willoughby, Lady Eliza, Fitz, Thornbury, and McGregor in attendance, it was all becoming rather too real.

But it was too late to question his decision now.

The vicar appeared both perplexed and curious, which was natural since no one had known that the duke who lived so close to their town was even interested in marrying, let alone had a woman in mind – and one who was here, at his estate. There was also the entire business of the special license, although Levi was hoping the man wouldn't question their marriage and its validity.

Luckily, being a duke did come with a few advantages as the vicar simply began to read from the text.

And in just a few minutes, Levi was a married man.

* * *

SIENA WAS both freezing and flushed throughout her body as she and Levi were pronounced husband and wife. Had that truly just happened? She, the woman who had run from a wedding just weeks ago, was now married to a different man?

If someone had told her a short time ago that she would have any part in such a tale, she would have laughed in surprise.

But here they were.

Eliza and Lord Fitzroy filled the stunned silence with exclamations of congratulations, while Siena found that she could look anywhere but at Levi.

She had shared the most intimate parts of herself with

him, completely trusted him with all of her secrets, her feelings, her body – but she had protected her heart, shielding it from him. Until today. Now she was most afraid that she was about to lose it anyway.

Before she had to say a word, however, she was interrupted by the sound of the door banging open. They looked at one another in horror, and soon enough the front foyer was filled with men – noblemen, yes, but others who looked around in concern as they likely hadn't realized they would be rescuing Siena from the arms of a duke – especially a duke who did not seem to be holding Siena in any form of distress.

"Can I help you, Lord Sterling?" Levi said, stepping forward in front of Siena.

"I have come to collect my daughter, and there is nothing you can do about it," Lord Sterling sneered. "I have enough of my friends here with me who can testify as to what happened here. My daughter will return to where she belongs."

"Actually," Levi said as calmly as he could, even though his heart was racing at the number of people who had invaded his home, all staring at him as though he was a ghastly beast. He had nearly reached for his sword, so leery he was about the threat. "You have no authority over Siena anymore."

"I am her father."

"That may be," Levi said, straightening now, for he finally had claim to something he was proud of. "But I am her husband now, which, I believe, takes precedence."

They were all silent for a moment, taking in this new piece of information, until Lord Sterling began to laugh, although no one echoed him besides a few half-hearted chuckles from his followers.

"That is not possible," he finally said when he stopped for air. "I saw you both mere hours ago and you certainly weren't married."

"Things change."

"But—"

"If I may," the vicar, a small, timid man with a round face and glasses, stepped forward with a finger in the air. "They are actually married, according to the church and the law. I just completed the ceremony myself, by special license from the Archbishop of Canterbury."

"The Archbishop?" Lord Sterling said, his eyes nearly popping out of his head. "A special license? You cannot be serious."

"He is," Siena said softly, wishing that things were different, that it never had to come to this, that she had a family she could have trusted to see to her best interests. "We were married but a few moments before you arrived."

"It will be annulled."

"A duke's marriage, sanctioned by the Archbishop?" Levi said, raising his eyebrow. "I think not."

The men who surrounded Lord Sterling seemed uncertain of the next course of action. They shifted back and forth, their eyes flicking around the room.

"Stay here," Levi said in Siena's hair as he walked toward Lord Sterling, only he didn't look at the man himself, but rather at all of those who had followed him here. He had to fight the urge to back away from them all, to hide elsewhere in this estate he had made his home, but he had promised to protect Siena, and protect her he would, even if it meant showing his face and accepting the horrified reactions.

He knew that Lord Sterling was beyond listening to any reason, but he had a feeling that he could implore to the other men's sense of hierarchy, or if not, he could, at the very least, scare them off.

"If any of you dare to challenge the marriage of the Duke of Dunmore – or the Duke of Death if you prefer – then take it to the House of Lords, if you wish. But we have a special license from the Archbishop of Canterbury himself, and

Lady Siena is now my wife. You can refer to her as Your Grace."

He smiled then, which he knew would appear rather sinister, so forced it was along with the scar that pulled at his cheek when he did so.

"Any questions?"

There didn't appear to be any as no one said a word in return to him, but rather directed their questions to Lord Sterling.

"My lord, I don't believe there is anything we can do," one of the men said, leaning forward to speak in his ear. "We cannot take the girl by force, and she does not appear willing to leave."

"Fall in love with your captor, did you, girl?" Lord Sterling said, leaning in toward her. "You are making a big mistake."

"You are wrong, Father," Siena answered, her voice soft yet filled with strength. "I am choosing to do something for myself, just as I did when I ran from my wedding. Only this time, I have decided that I will not run anymore, but, rather, am going to stand up for myself and decide my own fate."

Even as her father blustered, Levi was filled with an immense sense of pride as he realized that she was right, and that, perhaps, he had something to learn from her.

These men in front of him had grimaced at his face, yes, but what did it matter? It was only his problem if he *allowed* them to affect him, but the people of significance – Siena, most specifically – didn't care about his scars, nor what he looked like.

He had faced them – for her – but perhaps he could even learn to face them for himself.

"Leave," he said, waving his hand forward. "And this time, don't come back."

CHAPTER 24

"Well, that was all rather dramatic," Lady Willoughby said after Siena's father and his men had disappeared down the front drive.

He had obviously been reluctant to leave, but with the other men too uncertain to follow through on his orders, he had eventually had no choice.

"Too dramatic," Siena agreed.

She was standing with the two women in the front foyer while Levi and Lord Fitzroy followed a distance behind her father to make certain that they actually disappeared off of the property.

The truth was, she was rather nervous to spend time with Levi again. When they had previously been alone, before they had wed, it had been temporary, both of them having the option to continue on with their lives, but now – now they were tied together forever.

"You are a married woman, Siena," Eliza said, echoing her thoughts. "How do you feel?"

"I hardly know how I feel," she said, fluttering her hand in front of her. "So much has happened in such a short amount of time."

"Well, we will leave you to your new husband," Lady Willoughby said with a knowing smile. "It has been wonderful to spend time with you, Siena, and to become acquainted with the duke. While I wish this had all played out somewhat differently, in the end, I think you have found the path you were supposed to follow."

"I hope so," Siena said with a forced smile, trying to hide her nerves.

"I shall hopefully see you soon, Siena," Eliza said, stepping forward and throwing her arms around her. "I do love you."

"And I you, Eliza," she said. "Thank you for everything that you have done for me."

"Of course," Eliza said, squeezing her tight. "Who knows – there might be a day when you will return the favor."

Their carriage came around from the stables, pulling in front of the house. After the footmen had loaded their valises, Eliza and her mother stepped up into the carriage, waving their farewells. Siena had to wipe a tear away from her face as she watched the coach trundle down the drive – followed by a footman riding the horse she had "borrowed."

She wondered how long it would be until she would see Eliza again. She could hardly imagine Levi wanting to venture into London anytime soon, and he hadn't exactly enjoyed having guests here at the estate. Would he welcome them back?

Siena appreciated his commitment to her more than he would ever know, and yet she couldn't help the small part of her that realized there would be some major sacrifices to be made – including her connections to the world beyond the estate's doors.

Needing a moment, she collected herself with a sigh, noting that the sun was beginning to lower beyond the horizon. Just enough time, she considered, for a walk through the rose garden.

The long grass whispered against her skirts as she crossed the field toward the grove of trees. For the first time in a long time, she felt safe, free, knowing that no one would be coming after her and that, by marrying her, Levi had ensured that she had free will for the first time in her life.

All else aside, she knew that, no matter what, he would never make her do or be anyone she chose not to be, for which she would be forever grateful.

The chirping of birds and buzzing of insects filled the air, the rustling of leaves and the occasional snap of twigs under her feat adding to the music around her. This was beautiful, she considered, and she would never again take it for granted, knowing what kind of life would have awaited her had she remained in London.

She smelled the roses before she saw them, and she knew, then, that no matter what happened, the scent would always remind her of Levi and the love he had shown her in his sacrifice – even if he didn't actually feel so strongly for her in truth.

She hugged her shawl closely around her, so caught up in her feelings that she wasn't as aware of her surroundings as she should have been.

Which was why she was completely taken by surprise when the strong arms looped around her back, covering her mouth and dragging her away before she even had a chance to scream.

* * *

"I'm glad to see the last of them," Levi said as he and Fitz watched the dust from the retreating horses and carriage continue down the road.

"I always thought it was a blessing that you were so close to London, but perhaps it was the opposite," Fitz said. "It made it easy for Sterling to return. You were married with very little time to spare."

"Well, I suppose it also allowed you to visit and complete your journey to Canterbury in time," Levi said.

"Look at you, becoming the optimist," Fitz said with a grin, and Levi snorted and shook his head at him.

"I am actually glad to be married to Siena, believe it or not."

"I do believe it," Fitz returned. "She is not only beautiful, but she is sweet and she puts up with your grumpy self."

"Enough talk of her like that," Levi grunted, which had Fitz laughing.

"Easy now, I have no romantic notions upon her," he said. "Just admiring you and your marriage."

"Do not get too jealous quite yet," Levi said sardonically. "It's barely even started yet."

"What is your plan now?" Fitz asked as his horse pawed the ground impatiently below him.

"Now, I will return to my wife," he said. "The marriage was so hasty that I am afraid she is rather questioning of my motives as well as my feelings. I must make her comfortable."

"Will we be seeing you in London at all?" Fitz asked, raising a brow.

"I'm not sure," Levi admitted. "If Siena would like to return, then perhaps."

If it would make her happy, then so be it.

"Good to hear it," Fitz said. "On that note, this is where we will say our farewells."

"You are leaving?" Levi said in surprise.

"Yes. My saddlebags are packed. You should be alone with your bride, at least for a time. But don't get too comfortable – I will return for a visit soon."

"I'm counting on it," Levi said, realizing it was the first time he had ever told Fitz that he actually enjoyed his visits and would like him to repeat them. "Listen, Fitz," he began, trying to find the right words to tell his friend how much he appreciated all that he had done for him.

"I know, I am the best friend anyone could ever have," Fitz said with a cheeky grin, understanding. "You are lucky that I never gave up on you, despite your surly ways. And you will appreciate me forever."

"Something like that," Levi said, unable to help his laugh. "I shall see you soon, I expect."

"You couldn't get rid of me if you tried – you should know that by now," Fitz said, and with that, he rode away, as Levi turned his horse around to go find his bride.

He pushed Lucky hard on the way home, eager to return to Siena. He had made love to her before, yes, but this time was going to be different. This time, he could take his time, savour her, knowing that he had every day, every night for the rest of their lives to explore her. He could focus on more than simply enjoying the moment, but instead, be patient, willing, understanding, and enjoy every moment she granted him.

He just had to convince her that what he felt for her was enough, that he could be that man she needed.

The moment he rounded the drive, the hairs on the back of his neck stood high, and there was almost an eerie silence in the air, absent of the calls of the animals and the birds that should have been there. The wind rustled in the trees, but instead of a calming breeze, it made his hair stand on end. He couldn't say exactly what was off, but he was reminded of the day he had come upon Siena when she had been caught by the highwaymen.

He pushed Lucky even harder up the drive, swinging off

of the horse before he had come completely to a stop. He ran up the steps, pushing open the front door and calling Siena's name as he took his first steps in the house.

"Siena!" he shouted, filled with a desperation to see her, to know that he had no reason to be on edge. "Siena!"

"Oh, Your Grace, thank goodness you are here," Thornbury said, rushing to the door. The butler was out of breath, one hand on his chest. "Lady Siena, that is, Her Grace, she – she is gone."

"What do you mean, gone?" Levi growled.

"After you left, she was with the other ladies. And then Lady Willoughby and Lady Eliza departed in their carriage. Through the upstairs window, I saw Her Grace walking toward the rose garden but, the next thing I knew, she was being carried away down the front drive."

"Carried? By whom?"

"She was on horseback, but I couldn't see who was with her. By the time Collins managed to saddle a horse to take off after her, it was too late."

Thank goodness Lucky was already saddled. Levi knew exactly where she had gone and who had taken her – her father.

"Find McGregor!" he called out to Thornbury, hoping that his valet could accompany him to provide him assistance, but Thornbury was holding his hands in the air as his greyish black hair stood on end.

"We can't find him either," he said. "We tried, as we were looking for all the help we could, but we have no idea what has become of him."

"Very well. No time to wait for him," Levi said, before swinging up on Lucky and taking off.

"Where are you going?" Thornbury called out, and Levi turned, his words flying over his shoulder.

"To London!"

London. The one place he had said he'd never return. But for Siena, he would go anywhere.

CHAPTER 25

Siena was doing all within her power to stay calm.

She knew that Levi would find her and would rescue her. He had proven time and again he would go beyond any impossibility to protect her, which left her no doubt that he would find her. She just had to stay safe until he did. As safe as possible in this barren, dark, damp room, trapped alone with her captor.

"Why are you doing this?" Siena implored, the rope that bound her to a rickety wooden chair biting into her wrists when she twisted from side to side. "I thought that you were his friend."

"So did he."

"But why—"

"He doesna deserve my friendship."

"How can you say that?"

McGregor grimaced. "He took everything from me. He might not have realized it, but he ruined my life."

"Everything? What do you mean?" Siena said, confused even in her panic. "He was your officer in the army. He told me that your family was gone, that you had no one to return to. He gave you a job, a home, a—"

"He did. And I appreciated that, yes. But then, just when I found the one person who could mean something to me, could become my family, he took him away from me."

"Who?"

"His brother."

"What do you mean?" Siena asked, needing to know despite her predicament.

McGregor looked away, his face twisting uncomfortably. "Never mind. It doesn't matter."

"You became Levi's valet when he lived with his brother at the entailed estate, did you not?"

"I did."

"Did the former duke mean something to you?" Siena asked, noting the grief that filled McGregor's eyes when she mentioned Levi's brother. "I can understand the loss of a friend, yes, but—"

"He was more than a friend."

"Oh." She paused for a moment as the realization dawned on her, as shocking as it was. "I am sorry for your loss, McGregor, but it wasn't Levi's fault. He loved his brother. He tried to save him."

"Then how did he walk away from the fire?" McGregor burst out. "It's not right. It should have been Levi who died."

The way he made his accusation tugged at something in Siena's mind, and she narrowed her eyes at him through the dark, dusty air. "What do you mean that it *should have been Levi?*" she questioned, peering up at him. "Did you have something to do with the fire?"

He shifted his gaze away from her, looking from one side to the other. "No."

"You did," she said, leaning forward in the chair as best

she could, her entire body on edge. "How could you do such a thing?"

"He wasn't supposed to be in there," McGregor choked out, his back plastered against the wall behind him as he doubled over. "It was only supposed to be Lord Levi."

"Why would you try to kill your lover's brother?" she asked, even as her heart began to pound faster with the extra shock that the man who had captured her was capable of killing another.

"Because he knew too much of my past," McGregor said, his face twisting almost evilly. "He provided me a job as a valet, but the duke would never have continued with me had he known some of the things I did."

"You did them in war," Siena said, even though she had no idea why she was trying to console the man who had tried to kill Levi. She supposed some habits were hard to erase. "Be that as it may," she continued, summoning her courage, "Levi didn't kill his brother. You did."

"I did not!" McGregor roared. "The duke was only there because Lord Levi had asked to speak with him. About me. And then he arrived late to their meeting. It was his fault entirely."

"Or so you have convinced yourself," Siena said softly. "I can understand that is probably how you have been able to live with what you did."

"He escaped death, but instead he locked himself away in that estate, refusing to spend any time in the world, hiding because of what? A few scars? His brother would never have been so vain."

"I believe his scars are a reminder of what happened," Siena said quietly, knowing it was not his appearance which hid Levi away, but rather the constant reminder of how they had occurred.

McGregor only growled, and Siena took this as the opportunity to ask what she really needed to know.

"Why take me? What difference does that make? Is this one of those 'if I can't have love, then no one can' type of situations?"

"Somewhat," McGregor grumbled. "But there is more to it. Do you not recognize where you are?"

Siena looked around her, peering into the darkness. She had been dragged here with a burlap bag over her head, so she had been unable to see anything, although she suspected from the length of time it had taken them to journey here that they were in London. After McGregor had hauled her onto a horse for a few minutes, they had met a waiting carriage. The drive had been silent and uncomfortable despite the elegance she could feel of the carriage below her.

Saltwater and fish had filled the air as they had walked from the carriage into this building, along with an unmistakable rot that signified the Thames. When they had stepped into the building, a musty smell hinted at its age and abandonment.

He had removed the bag once they were within, but there was nothing to see but worn, wooden walls and scarred flooring. The place was empty. Even the windows were so grimy that she couldn't see out of them to what she was sure was the river beyond as she could hear both the water as well as the clopping of hooves on the other side.

"Why would you bring me all the way to London?" she demanded. "Why not just take care of this at the estate?"

"Because I struck a deal," he said with a sigh, as though it troubled him to have done so.

"My father," she said with a breath, realizing the truth, her heart sinking as any belief she had in her family fled completely.

"I first shared your presence with him and then when I

learned of his plight on his first visit to Greystone, I was better prepared for his return. I followed him and told him that I would deliver you to him for a price."

Ire began to simmer in Siena's belly that her father would stoop to such lowness, although at least it was more likely that her life was not at risk if he had arranged this.

"What am I worth to you, then?" she asked.

"The duke's life."

So much for the panic having dissipated.

"What is that supposed to mean?" she demanded, but he was already backing away, shaking his head.

"I have said too much."

"You have said nothing at all. Do you really think that Levi is going to exchange himself for me?"

"Absolutely. Your father will not have to worry about you seeking an annulment – for your husband will be gone." He paused. "Not that I care if you survive this or not, but your father would prefer you do."

Well, that was something, at least.

"What is there to survive?" she forced herself to choke out.

He reached into his pocket and pulled out a tinder box. When the flame arose, his eyes glinted with it, the grin crossing his face so malicious that it caused Siena's entire body to shake. She realized then that there was more to McGregor's malice than she would have thought.

"It was you," she breathed. "The fire in the stables."

"It was," he said with a flourish. "Not my finest work, but then, the exterior of the building was not as flammable as I would have liked."

"Y-you are cruel," she stammered out. She had heard of evil within people of course, but never had she actually seen it.

He shrugged, unaffected by her words. "Call me what you want. We all get our joy from different places."

"Did the former duke know about this joy you found?" Siena asked. "What did he think of it?"

"He knew nothing of it," McGregor scoffed. "How could he?" He began pacing back and forth, his agitation growing. "Enough of all these questions. Your father should be here by now."

"I actually doubt it."

"Of course he will!" McGregor burst out. "That was the plan! Then I will receive my money and my vengeance."

"He will not return me to the household until he knows that my marriage is annulled or…" or she was widowed. But she couldn't say that aloud, for she didn't want to put the idea into the air. "I suppose you are my jailkeeper for now."

"I am no such thing," McGregor said haughtily, just as she hoped he would. "Stay here. I will go find him myself."

Siena raised a brow, wishing she could see the reaction when he realized that the viscount would not appear and sully himself until he knew that this had all been taken care of.

"Don't. Move," the valet commanded, pointing a finger at her, before he backed out of the door and shut it behind him. Siena listened to see how he might lock it, but from the scrapes and grunts she heard, it seemed as though he had, instead, pushed a piece of furniture against it, preventing her from opening the door.

Left alone, Siena crumpled to the ground, all of the strength that had been keeping her upright flooding away from her as she no longer felt the need to keep up the façade of fearlessness. For the truth was, she was terrified. Terrified that Levi wouldn't find her in time. Terrified that McGregor would succeed in killing him. Terrified that her father would find a way to interfere and ensure that her marriage was annulled.

It was a marriage that she hadn't even realized she had wanted.

But one that she would now fight with all her might to keep.

* * *

Levi thundered through the front door and through Lord Sterling's townhouse, practically pushing aside servants or men of business who stood in his path.

"Where is she?" he bellowed as he slammed open the viscount's study door.

Lord Sterling jumped, which momentarily satisfied Levi, before his expression turned into a sneer, as though he had seen off-putting food.

"What are you doing here?"

"I've come for my wife."

"Lost her already, have you?" the viscount bit out. "Did she finally see your entire face? Or does the rest of you match that scar and one look sent her running?"

Levi allowed the words to flow over him, imagining them sliding down his back, just as Siena had said they should.

"If you have allowed anything to happen to her—" he growled out, but the viscount held up a hand to stop him.

"Then you will do what? Others might be scared of the Duke of Death, but I assure you that I am not. Besides, what I do with my daughter should not concern you."

"She is my wife now," Levi said, even the thought of it causing a warm glow to wash over him. "If you commit any crime against her, then you are committing one against me."

As he finished, a woman stepped into the doorway of the

room. She looked like Siena, only older, colder, and far less joyful.

When she saw Levi, she stopped and visibly shivered, her lips puckering in disgust.

"Do we have a visitor, my lord?" she asked her husband, but he waved her away.

"No one worth concerning yourself with," he said, but Levi stepped forward and smiled.

"I would be your son-in-law," he said, enjoying the look of horror that crossed Siena's mother's face. "The Duke of Dunmore."

"Son-in-law?" she exclaimed. "How—"

"Siena has done something stupid, but I am fixing it," Lord Sterling muttered. "Do not concern yourself."

"Where. Is. She." Levi's patience had run thin, and he was ready to show this man what it meant to cross him, consequences be damned.

"She's not here," the viscount said with a sigh. "But I have an idea of where she is. I will take you to her."

Levi narrowed his eyes, immediately suspicious. "What is your plan here?"

"I have no plan," the viscount said, shrugging his shoulders. "She came with me willingly. In fact, when I returned for her, she practically begged me to take her with me. Said that she had made a huge mistake, that she could not imagine herself tied to such a man for the rest of her life. I promised her that I would have the marriage annulled, and she could be free to live the life she wished."

"With Lord Mulberry?"

"Why yes, as it happens, Siena did come to her senses and agree to marry him. Once she is done with you, of course."

"Oh, thank heaven," Lady Sterling said, placing a hand over her heart. "I have barely been able to show my face in society ever since that debacle."

"You both disgust me," Levi bit out, understanding now why his scars had never bothered Siena.

It was because she had grown up with true beasts who had nothing on his scars.

"You are lying. And I am going to prove it."

He pushed past the viscount, ignoring his shocked outcry and his wife's call for the servants. Instead, Levi stalked through the house, pushing open every door, questioning every servant. "Siena!" he called out. "Siena, where are you?"

"There is no one here," the viscount said smugly, filling the doorway behind him. "I will, however, tell you that she is in a building near the Thames. It should not take you long to find her, if you ride as fast as you did here."

Lord Sterling held out a small piece of paper, which Levi snatched from him to read the address upon it.

He knew that this was far too easy, that this was most certainly a trap of some sort. He wasn't stupid. The viscount would probably be happy to see him dead so that Siena was no longer tied to a marriage with him.

But he would have to take the chance.

For he would do anything to save his bride.

CHAPTER 26

Siena had nearly fallen asleep, so exhausted was she after her ordeal, but every time her eyes closed, the ropes would cut into her wrists and she would be startled back awake. McGregor had, at this point, nodded off himself, but when she heard the shouts coming from outside the door, she hoped he would stay sleeping.

"Siena!"

Levi. He was here.

She strained to catch a glimpse of him through the windows, but she couldn't see anything through the filth.

McGregor rose, sputtering, to attention – apparently, he had picked up a few skills during wartime – and snapped up the gun sitting beside him.

"Time to say farewell to your darling husband," he said with an evil grin, opening the door to peek out around it. Siena's heart jumped in hope when he cursed.

"Stay here!" he ordered as if she had any choice in the matter.

Her heart pounded as she wished with all of her might that the only person she would see walk through that door was Levi. As for McGregor or her father, she would be perfectly happy if she never saw either of them again.

"Levi!" she called out, trying to stand, but it was no use – she was tied to the chair too tightly. She looked around her for anything that she might be able to use to free herself, but the room was empty.

Although some of the splinters of wood might be worth a shot.

She used all of her might to inch her chair forward, her eyes focused and determined as she tried to imagine that she was a heroine in one of the books she read, only she refused to be one that walked stupidly into danger and then sat and waited for her prince to rescue her. She had every belief that Levi could and would save her, but she was equally intent on doing all she could to make it as easy for him as possible.

Angling the chair over, she lifted her wrists and scraped them against the splintered wood, although just as she did, she heard shouting from outside. Knowing that she might have precious little time, she lifted her hands up and down, harder, faster, hoping the rope would rip sooner rather than later.

Her heart was in her throat when she heard the commotion from beyond the door, and she urged herself on faster. That, however, did nothing to help her as the chair tipped over with her momentum and she went flying forward, unable to catch herself as she landed on her side with a painful "oof."

Ignoring the throbbing in her hip, she tried to inch herself backward to continue her work, hopeful when it seemed that her hands were a little looser.

Perhaps she could do this after all.

That's when she smelled the first hint of smoke.

And panic burned within her.

* * *

Levi could hardly believe his eyes at the building that stretched up in front of him.

He had known that many of the buildings along the Thames were rather derelict, but this one looked as though it was ready to fall over at any moment.

Anger spurred him forward as he rode up to the door, giving Lucky a pat and a promise to reward him for all of his hard work before tying him on the rail away from the building.

"Siena!" he called, his heart pounding as he knew there was no way that she was here alone, that someone had to have forced her here. He could only pray that she had been left unharmed.

His boots had just hit the bottom stair when the door swung open, the barrel of a gun the first thing he saw.

Relief flooded through him when he saw the identity of its holder.

"McGregor!" he said, wondering how his valet could possibly have arrived before him but grateful, nonetheless. "Thank goodness. You found Siena. How is she? Is she all right? Is she injured?"

"She is fine," McGregor said, a strange expression twisting his face. "For now."

"What do you mean?" Levi asked as a surprising sense of unease crept over him. "What is happening, McGregor? Where is Siena?"

He began to push past his annoyingly confusing valet to find his wife, but McGregor shocked the hell out of him when he dug the pistol into his ribs.

"Stop."

"Stop? You are aware that you answer to me," Levi said, hating to pull such rank, but he did pay the man's salary after all. The least McGregor could do was provide him the explanation for why he couldn't enter the building.

"Not anymore," McGregor said, his expression twisting his face to the point that Levi hardly recognized him.

"Move. Aside." Levi would determine what had so changed McGregor later, but for right now, he had to find Siena.

"I don't think you understand," McGregor said, lifting the shotgun now and pointing it at Levi's head. "You are not going inside. You are here for an altogether different reason."

"McGregor, have you gone mad?" Levi growled, his impatience and disbelief mounting. "Did someone pay you to turn against me? Lord Sterling?"

"Yes, as it happens, but it didn't take much convincing," McGregor said, butting him with the shotgun and forcing him backwards, walking him all the way to the bank of the river. The waves lapped behind him, and Levi disjointedly wondered if he was going to shoot him here. It would make for an easy clean up.

"Nor am I going to follow through on my end of the deal. You see, I've been waiting a long time for this opportunity. I never thought the day would come. You were miserable – the way it should have been. But then I see you walking around with a smile on your face, a spring in your step." He let out an inhuman bellow. "I couldn't take it anymore!"

Levi was stunned into silence, wondering where this man had come from, how McGregor had lived with him, helped to take care of him, been one of his closer friends, and yet harbored so much hatred against him.

"McGregor, what did I ever do to you?" he asked disconnectedly. "We served together. When you had no one to return to, I gave you a job, a home."

"It was all fine until you killed him," he answered, his voice filled with vehemence.

"Killed who?"

"Your brother."

Pain washed over Levi in a wave, as well as all of those feelings of guilt that had consumed him over the past year. It seemed Siena's words had somehow gotten through, however, for it was not quite as dark as it had been in the past – more grief than guilt this time.

"I didn't kill him," Levi said quietly, having an inkling of what had caused such pain in McGregor. He had guessed his brother preferred his own sex, not that it was something they had ever spoken about. It did explain a lot. "I did everything I could to save him. I am sorry that you have felt such loss. I understand it more than you know."

"You understand nothing," McGregor growled out. "But you will."

Ice seized Levi's heart when he realized just what he meant.

"McGregor," he said, holding his hands up. "Taking love away from someone else does not bring back your own."

"No. But it will make you feel the same pain that I do."

Levi looked down at McGregor's hands, deciding he couldn't waste any more time. He lunged forward to take the shotgun from him, but as he did, McGregor released it, and the momentum sent Levi flying forward. He fell on his left side with a grunt, his burned shoulder and hip taking most of the pain. Pushing it aside, he rose to his knees, needing to get to his feet.

But before he could do so, pain burst into his skull, sending stars in front of his eyes, and then everything went black.

* * *

THE SMOKE ROLLED into the room before the fire did.

Siena stayed as low as she could – easy to do when she was already on the floor. But then the heat followed, and she began to sweat, both from its effects as well as the fear that she was never going to escape this.

"Good thoughts, Siena, good thoughts," she murmured to herself as she closed her eyes and envisioned the rope tying her hands together ripping in half – which, shockingly and thankfully, it did, sending her hands flying to the sides as she cried out in relief. She pushed herself up and untied her feet, although it took much longer than she would have liked, her hands numb from being tied so tightly.

That time proved far too valuable, as when she ran, nearly tripping, to the door of the room she was being held in, she placed her hand over it and found it was hot to the touch. She knew that was not a good sign, but there was no other way out of this room. It was to chance it or to die.

She pushed through the door, nearly sobbing to find that the fire was much stronger here in the front room. The exit was blocked, and the windows too small for her to fit through.

She was never going to escape.

As the flames consumed the old wooden building, panic rose in Siena's chest, along with the smoke that was filling her lungs. She coughed and sputtered, her eyes stinging from the acrid fumes. The heat was unbearable, scorching her skin even through the layers of her dress.

Amidst the terror, through the window she caught a glimpse of Levi – but instead of relief she only felt additional terror. He was lying prostrate on the ground, blood seeping out of a wound on the back of his head. As she watched him, it was almost as though he felt her gaze, for he groaned and turned over before his eye flew open, his expression changing from one of pain to horror as he pushed himself off the ground as quickly as he likely could, using his hands on his thighs to do so.

He had obviously been injured in some way himself, and Siena's heart throbbed anew that he had been hurt.

"Siena!" he shouted, his voice barely audible over the crackling fire. She tried to call out to him, but her throat was raw, her voice lost in the din of the inferno.

With tears streaming down her face, Siena stumbled through the burning building, avoiding the growing flames, each step feeling like a mile. The walls groaned and creaked around her, threatening to collapse at any moment. She knew she had to find an escape, but the smoke made it impossible to see.

Even through her cloying panic, all she could think about was how this must be Levi's worst nightmare coming true again. She had to come out from this alive, if only so that his own inner demons wouldn't destroy him.

For if she was lost to the fire, she knew that he would never recover.

CHAPTER 27

Levi came back to the present with a groan.

His hand sought the back of his head, coming away sticky and red when he touched the spot where he had been hit, likely with the shotgun.

Not that it mattered. Not anymore.

He blinked, trying to clear the fog from his eye as he raised his head, horrified to see the building in front of him ablaze – the building where he was fairly certain Siena was being held.

He could have sworn he caught sight of her through the window, floating like a ghost within the building.

Let her be alive, he screamed within himself, forgetting the throbbing pain in his head as he pushed himself to his feet.

The fire was taunting him, telling him that he could never overcome it, that it was going to claim another victim – but he squared his shoulders and started ahead with determination.

He was going to save Siena. Or he would die trying. It was him against the fire and only one of them would win this time.

He surged toward the building, moving as fast as he could, ignoring his injuries, leaving the pain behind. He had wallowed in the pain long enough. It was time to forge a new path ahead. The front door was engulfed in flames, so he decided to move to the side of the building where he had either seen Siena or a mirage.

Creaks and groans sounded around him, and he knew he had to work fast. He pushed toward a window, bellowing as he gripped the wooden boards in front of him and ripped them away to widen the window enough that he could fit through.

When he entered the building, the strange yet unfortunately familiar whooshing sound surrounded him, cracks and pops accentuating the eery air.

Fear gripped him like icy claws, and he was nearly unable to move. The heat was unbearable, and doubt filled him as memories that were more like nightmares from the past resurfacing in the forefront of his mind, reminding him that he had failed before – would he fail again? He had thought that losing his brother was the worst thing that could ever happen to him, but if he lost Siena too, he wasn't sure how he could ever live with himself.

He also knew that he didn't have much time.

"Siena!" he tried to call out, his voice already raw from the smoke. "Siena!"

He stumbled forward, his foot slipping on the ground – only, it wasn't the ground. It was pale pink fabric.

"My God," he cried out in both prayer and supplication.

His heart beat even faster in panic when he saw her lying there, her eyes closed, her arm flung out in front of her. He wasn't sure how long she had been in here nor the amount of time he had been unconscious, but she likely had inhaled too much smoke.

With a start and a curse, he realized flames were licking at the hem of her dress. He beat them out with his hands, uncaring that he was singeing both his palms.

He lifted her, swinging her over his shoulder, the simplest and fastest way to carry her out of this inferno. As he ran back the way he came, he had to dodge falling debris, and soon he worried that he would be too late – that the window would have literally closed.

But there it was – a glimpse of the darkening sky beyond. He surged through the opening, falling onto the gravel before them, ignoring the rocks pricking his body as he rolled them side to side, extinguishing any flames that had followed them out.

When he finally realized the heat had subsided and the immediate danger had passed, he lifted Siena a few yards away and laid her on the ground, wanting to shake her back to him but knowing that she needed much gentler care.

"Siena," he called out desperately. "Siena, can you hear me?"

Despite his despair, his experience from war returned to him and he acted without thought, checking to make sure that nothing was blocking her from receiving all of the fresh air she required, which should hopefully be enough to restore her breathing.

At least she *was* still breathing – although it was far too ragged for his liking.

He ran his hands over her body, checking her for burns, terrified she would be subjected to the same pain he had lived with for the past year, but breathed a deep sigh of relief to discover that only her dress had been singed and none of her perfect skin.

A hand touched his shoulder and he flinched, pulling back his fist as he turned, but it was only a man who likely lived or worked near the docks, his hands up in front of him in defense from Levi's harsh stature.

It was then Levi noticed that an entire crowd had formed around them, drawn by the blaze, many working to extinguish it, using the water from the river, buckets, and a hand-pumped fire-fighting contraption that was being pulled toward them.

A woman appeared next to him with a canvas drawstring bag in her hands. "I can help," she said. "I might not be a physician but as close to one as you might find at the moment."

Levi paused, wondering if he should accept her help or if she would only make things worse, but finally, he relented. He'd stop her if anything seemed suspicious.

But all she did was pull a brown bottle from her bag, holding it in front of Siena's nose as scents of sage and lavender rose in the air. Siena twitched slightly a few times, but her eyes remained closed, leaving Levi to wonder whether or not they had actually done anything.

But then Siena stirred, coughing, and the first word she spoke with her eyes still closed was his name.

"Levi," she groaned out. "Levi, where are you?"

"Here, love," he said, pulling her into his lap, wrapping his arms around her far tighter than he likely should have, but he just couldn't seem to let her go. "I'm right here beside you."

"I'm so sorry," she murmured, blinking as she looked up into his eyes, and he could only shake his head before he swallowed down his emotion a few more times.

"There is nothing to be sorry for."

"You had to go into the fire."

"I would go anywhere for you," he said, leaning in close, wiping away her tears. "Don't you know that?"

"But the fire—"

"Didn't take you. And that's all that matters."

"McGregor—"

"We'll worry about him later," he said, needing her to rest

her voice, her throat, as he gathered her and tried not to think about how close he had been to losing her. "He will not get away with this."

His own throat tightened at the man's betrayal. Levi had thought he had given McGregor a new life, but he had been so consumed in his own misery that he hadn't realized what was happening around him.

"It's not your fault," she managed, her voice still hoarse as she seemed to read his mind. He began shaking his head, but her eyes bore into him. "It's not."

With that she gripped his forearms. "Take me home, Levi, please?"

Home. For the first time, the manor that had once seemed so cold and empty truly did feel like home, as it was now a place they shared together.

"Of course," he said, rising, relieved to see that while the blaze wasn't completely extinguished it did, at least, appear to be contained to the building and not spreading. He wished he could thank all of the people who were working so hard to protect the rest of the neighborhood, but at the moment, he needed to focus on his wife. "The problem is we only have Lucky, who I rode incredibly hard to get here. We can take him to Fitz's and borrow horses and a carriage to return home, if you don't mind?"

She nodded and leaned into him as he supported her toward Lucky who remained ever loyal, despite the chaos that surrounded him. Levi gave him a good pat before helping Siena mount the horse and then leading him into the street, orienting himself toward Fitz's residence.

He would navigate them around less savory neighborhoods as best he could, but he was also well prepared to take on anyone who threatened.

As they traversed through London, he considered that this was the first time he had returned to the city since the fire that had taken his brother. He had hardly noticed any curious stares, and while it wasn't as though they were absent, he realized that he no longer cared, which was remarkable in itself.

He had, in more ways than one, gone through the fire and come out the other side.

He owed a great deal of it to Siena, that much was obvious. But he had also done much of the work himself, and he was proud of it.

For now, finally, he knew he was good enough for his wife.

And he was going to spend the rest of their lives proving it to her.

* * *

Siena was weary, every bone in her body suffering from exhaustion. It hurt to breathe, and her throat was raw.

But she was alive, with Levi's arms wrapped tightly around her. She never wanted to leave them.

At some point as they rode through London, he must have mounted Lucky behind her. She was so tired; she must have been near to falling off.

"Down we come," he said, helping her from the horse, lifting her in his arms as though she weighed nothing and carrying her up the steps of a townhouse.

He had just set her down when the door in front of them burst open, and a very surprised Fitz stood in the doorway with McGregor standing beside him.

Panic rose within her as Levi shouted at Fitz that McGregor was a danger, but Fitz only smiled that usual grin of his.

"I know. We've come to an understanding, haven't we, McGregor?"

The man snarled and tried to pull away from Lord Fitzroy, and it was only then that Siena belatedly saw the pistol that Fitz had dug into McGregor's side.

"When McGregor here realized that the two of you were still alive, too much of a crowd had gathered for him to finish the job. He assumed correctly you would make your way here, and seemed to think that he could wait for you in the shadows of my house. Isn't that right, McGregor?"

He only grunted in reply.

"Well, unfortunately for him, I am more capable than most believe. I found our friend lurking, and he eventually confessed to everything, so heated he was, weren't you? The authorities should be here soon."

"We have quite a story, Fitz," Levi said. "It's been a night."

"A story I look forward to hearing, but we have much to deal with first. What am I to tell the magistrate?"

Levi told him what had occurred as succinctly as possible, which had Lord Fitzroy swearing and then releasing a low whistle.

"I don't think it will take much convincing that McGregor is a threat," he said. "Off we go now. Dunmore, help yourself to any guest room of your choosing. Your wife looks ready to faint."

"Actually, if I could stable Lucky and borrow a horse and carriage to return home, I would be most grateful."

"Of course," Fitz said. "Whatever you need. And while it's not required, I would request that you return them and collect Lucky yourself, so that I might see you – both of you – again soon. Soothe my worry and all that."

"Look forward to it," Levi said, and when Siena peered at him, she realized that he actually meant it. Perhaps times were changing.

CHAPTER 28

By the time they returned to Greystone, Siena was fast asleep beside him. Levi gripped the potion that the medicine woman had given him. She had refused payment, telling him that a lovely young woman under such traumatic circumstances deserved to be healed, regardless of payment. Levi had still ensured that she had not walked away without some coin, and now he continued to bring the scented herbs to Siena's nose to help her breathe.

She didn't stir, but her breathing deepened and she stayed asleep as he carried her up to the front entrance.

"Your Grace!" Thornbury nearly immediately appeared, looking no less askew than he had before. He had one hand on his heart as he took in Levi with Siena safely in his arms, although Levi could only imagine how the two of them must appear. "You found Her Grace. Is she… is she—"

"She will be fine, Thornbury," he said, convincing himself as much as the butler. "She's had a scare and is exhausted, but she will recover."

"Thank goodness," the butler said just as the housekeeper appeared behind him. It seemed that she had heard everything that Levi had imparted, and she quickly began to bustle around, arranging all that she felt was required – food, drink, bath, Siena's maid – when all Levi really wanted was time alone with his wife, the opportunity to hold her and remind himself that she was no longer in any danger.

But he realized from the efforts of his staff just how much they had all come to love Siena, and so he allowed them all to do what they required to show their affection for her. It seemed far too long afterward that he was finally alone with her, on what, he realized belatedly, was their wedding night.

Siena had briefly awoken for her bath, but her eyes had remained closed nearly the entire time. Levi refused to leave the room, sending her maid out before he gently washed Siena's hair and her body, then lifted her from the bathtub, drying her and dressing her, with help from her sleepy movements, before tucking her into bed.

"What a day," he murmured as he reached out and drew her close to him. She still didn't wake, although she did nuzzle her body closer against his. He wrapped his arms around her, closed his eyes, and, for the first time in what felt like forever, easily fell asleep.

* * *

Siena woke the next morning stiff and sore, yet also complete and desperately happy. It took her a moment to remember why.

Then she recalled all that had occurred the previous day, from the wedding to the abduction to her father to McGregor, and she nearly became sick.

What had started as a beautiful morning had quickly turned to disaster, all due to the selfish actions of two men who couldn't see beyond their own circumstances.

Although it had ended as it began with Levi by her side – and really, what else mattered?

She opened her eyes to find him drowsily watching her, and she determined, then, to never let anyone and or anything interfere with what the two of them had found in one another.

"Levi?"

"Yes?"

She gripped his hands tightly. "I love you. So much."

The smile that broke out on his face – such a rare occurrence – warmed her right through.

"I love you too. More than you could ever know." He ran his hands over her cheeks. "How do you feel?"

"A bit stiff and sore, but better than I would have thought."

"When you were in that building, I…" He seemed at a loss for words, but Siena understood, for she had felt the exact same when she had seen him lying on the ground outside.

"I know," she said. "But all ended well, thank goodness."

"And now? Are you happy remaining here with me, knowing that your parents don't approve of us, that society will have questions?"

"Must you truly ask that?" she said, raising her eyebrows. "Do you forget that I ran away from the wedding that society was expecting? I don't care what anyone thinks, Levi. I'm here with you, and I will stay with you." She paused. "Thank you for coming for me. And for coming into the fire after me. I can only imagine how torturous that must have been."

"Yesterday made me realize that it is not the fire itself that scares me. It is the thought of losing someone to it. Yet now that we have overcome it, somehow it doesn't hold such power over me anymore."

"It is interesting, is it not, that the tragedy of losing your brother to fire only furthered McGregor's need for more fire, while it convinced you to avoid it completely?"

"I suppose that is the difference between setting the fire and being trapped within it."

"I suppose." She paused for a moment. "I do feel sorry for him."

Levi shook his head. "You are too kind. I cannot find it within myself to overcome what he did to you. What he did to my brother. Even through the circumstances."

"He is a troubled man, that is for certain."

Levi nodded before leaning in and kissing her gently, not wanting to injure her any further but needing the closeness.

Siena surprised him by reaching up and gripping his shirt, pulling him down toward her.

"Siena—"

"Make love to me," she whispered, needing him close to her, within her, but he was already leaning back away from her.

"It is too soon," he said. "I do not want to cause you any further harm."

She laughed lightly. "Trust me, what I have in mind will only make me feel better."

"Yes, but—"

"Please?" she said softly, her lips parting open as she was already nearly suffering with her need for him.

"Well, when you ask me like that…"

She laughed gleefully as she pulled him back toward her, fusing their lips together as she moved restlessly against him. They moved together slowly at first, as he treated her like porcelain, moving gently around her, not allowing any of his weight upon her.

She both appreciated it and longed for more, and finally she pushed against his chest until he rolled over and she swung her leg overtop of him to straddle him, then slowly sunk down upon him and set the pace herself.

He threw his head back, his open and vulnerable position sending a surge of power through her as they surrendered to one another and her fingers bit into his shoulders.

He pulsed within her as he found his release, sending her over the edge herself.

She finally rolled off him, and he stood from the bed, walking over to the washbasin and retrieving a piece of linen to gently clean her.

He had just returned to the bed to lay with her, giving her time to rest, when there was a knock on the door.

"Your Grace, you have a visitor," came the voice of Mrs. Porter.

"A visitor?" Siena called back. "Who is it?"

"Lady Eliza has returned."

"Oh dear," Siena said to Levi. "She must have heard about the abduction. Or the fire. Or both. I'm sorry, I know we were just married yesterday but—"

"Go put her mind at ease," he said. "I am not going anywhere."

Siena put herself together as best she could, seeing the bathtub but barely remembering her soak, before meeting Eliza in the drawing room, where her friend practically flung herself at her.

"Siena! My goodness, what happened to you? One moment I was leaving you a newly married woman and the next I hear that you were abducted and trapped in a fire? I cannot leave you for a moment before trouble finds you!"

Siena couldn't help but laugh as she returned Eliza's embrace and then led her over to the sofa.

"You are usually the one who puts me into trouble."

"Perhaps, but not this kind of trouble."

"You have a point," Siena said. "Sit down, for this is quite the story."

She told Eliza as much as she could, leaving out some of the details of Levi's own trauma, as well as McGregor's. She felt that wasn't for her to tell, even though she knew that Eliza would never share such secrets.

"And what of your father? How could he be involved in such a thing?"

Siena shrugged. "I suppose he only cared about his own reputation. He never meant for me to be hurt, I'm sure, but he certainly didn't care about Levi."

"My mother heard that your parents packed their London house and left for the country this morning, as though they were fleeing."

"They very likely were. I cannot see them wanting to stay and face any criticism."

"The good news is that likely means they have given up fighting your marriage. My mother also heard that Lord Mulberry has already set his intentions on a new bride."

"Oh, the poor thing," Siena said, but Eliza leaned in and placed a hand on her knee.

"That's just it," she said conspiratorially. "She is not young at all but a widow his own age."

"Is she really?"

"If my mother is correct," Eliza said.

"Your mother is always correct."

"This is true. She collects gossip better than anyone I have ever met."

They laughed slightly at that before Eliza leaned back and cast her eyes over Siena,

"I know you have been through an ordeal, but I must say, I have never seen you so happy."

"I have never *been* so happy," Siena said. "Thank you,

Eliza, for everything. If you hadn't helped me escape from my wedding, I can't even think about what I would be doing right now."

Eliza shuddered.

"You would not be with a man you love, that is for certain," she said, before holding Siena out at arm's length. "I should let you return to your new husband. Thank goodness you are so close to London. I don't think I could bear to have you live too far away."

"I completely understand," Siena returned. "Thank you for showing me what it means to have a voice. I shall see you soon, I hope."

"Of course. You will never be rid of me."

After a quick cup of tea, Eliza was about to leave when Levi appeared. Eliza curtseyed to him, but both women were surprised when Levi walked over and took her hands in his.

"You have been a very good friend to my wife," he said. "I will always appreciate that."

"You are a lucky man," she said before leaning in and quietly saying, "take good care of her."

"Always," he responded.

As Eliza's carriage disappeared, Siena walked forward and laid her head on Levi's chest. He wrapped an arm around her, and as Siena kissed the scarred side of his face, she realized that he no longer pulled back when she paid attention to that side of his body, not like he used to do.

"I'm so glad you saved me," she said, but he shook his head against her, the scruff on his chin lightly brushing against her forehead. She leaned in and inhaled the scent that was so uniquely him, which caused pleasure to shoot out to every limb of her body.

"You were the one who saved me," he said. "I could never have imagined that the decision to rescue you from those highwaymen would have changed the rest of my life."

"We saved each other then," she said. "I love you, Levi."
"And I love you."
He kissed her then, a searing promise of happiness.
Now, until forever.

EPILOGUE

"Are you certain about this?" Siena asked, looking up at Levi.

He set his jaw and nodded. "Absolutely."

They were in the carriage, headed for London – but they were not alone. Siena held their baby, Caroline, in her lap.

She was nearly a year now, and reached out for Levi as she always did when he was nearby.

"Papa!"

"I still do not think it's fair that was her first word," Sienna said, shaking her head.

"You did do most of the work."

"I did." She sighed. "But I must say, you are far more present in her life than most fathers are."

"Sometimes it's hard to believe that she loves me so much."

"Have I not taught you anything? You are far more loveable than you would ever believe."

"Still, I always thought she would be scared of me. Everyone is – except you."

Siena shook her head with a small smile on her face.

"Children are born to see the people they love as perfect. That's what you are to her."

"I hope I always will be."

It was a concern lodged deep within him – that someday, she would realize that her father was seen by the world as a monster.

"You will," Siena assured him. "For she knows the man you truly are. The man that I fall more in love with every day."

Levi treasured her words, as he did his wife, who was everything he had never known he had needed. She had become pregnant shortly after they had wed, and he had spent her entire pregnancy by her side, ensuring that she had everything she needed. Even now, he had yet to be apart from her and their daughter since the birth.

"Are you sure about this?" Siena asked once more as the carriage came to a halt.

"Absolutely."

He meant what he said as they pulled into London. He had finally decided to take his seat in the House of Lords – an action that he never would have thought possible before he had met Siena.

They arrived at the townhouse where they were going to make home for the Season. Siena herself had some trepidation, for the only time they had been in the city since she had been caught in the fire was the promised visit to return Fitz's horse and carriage. Levi was determined not to allow any of his own nerves to show, needing to be strong to support her.

They could have stayed at Greystone, of course, but often Parliament finished so late that Siena had feared Levi riding to them at such an hour. They would, however, return when there was a break in sessions.

Thornbury had travelled ahead to prepare the house – and the staff – for them. Levi had particular needs for his injuries, injuries that would never truly go away, while he knew Siena had also asked Thornbury to ensure that the staff was prepared to not allow Levi to feel any judgement.

He loved that she had done so, even if it was unnecessary. He was prepared for whatever was to come.

Thornbury greeted them with the enthusiasm of a man who hadn't seen them in years rather than a couple of weeks. Siena, of course, greeted each staff member by name once she was introduced, all while carrying Caroline on her hip, graciously declining when the nanny, who had accompanied them, offered to take her. Siena was a rather hands-on mother, which Levi loved her for, and it gave her purpose in her day.

By the time they had prepared for bed, he was exhausted, although most of it was from the nerves he was battling within rather than from anything he had actually experienced.

"Well?" Siena said, propping her head upon her hand. "Are you ready?"

"To take my place in the House? I believe so," he said, staring at the beautiful, long column of her neck. "I would prefer not to be here in London, but I also think that I must do as much good as I can in this world, and the best way to do that is to use the power that I have been bestowed. So here we are."

She leaned in and kissed him. "You will be absolutely wonderful."

He could only hope she was right.

* * *

When Levi prepared to leave the next evening, Siena was having trouble containing the nervous energy that filled her.

She helped him dress, choosing his clothes and even

tying his cravat, but when he stepped away from her toward the carriage, she knew she wouldn't be able to remain at home for hours on end and not know what was happening.

"I'm going with you," she announced, and he placed his hands on her upper arms.

"You cannot. Only titled men may enter the House of Lords."

"I understand that," she said, rolling her eyes. "But I want to come with you for the drive there."

"Why?"

"Why not?" she said with a shrug. "Caroline is sleeping, and I have nothing else to do. Once we have left you there, we will return home."

'Why am I not convinced?" Levi said, lifting a brow at her, but she knew that he was never able to deny her. "Very well. Hop in."

She clapped her hands together gleefully before ascending into the carriage.

Siena kept her hand on his leg the entire drive across London. She knew that he was nervous, even if he wouldn't show it. Ever the protector, he had tried to hide anytime his fears surfaced, but she could always tell by the twitch of his eye and the clenching of his jaw.

"I'm proud of you," she said, and he lifted a brow.

"For what? I haven't done anything."

"You are here," she said. "That is very brave." She leaned in. "You are not doing this for me, are you? Because you know that I would have been perfectly happy staying home at Greystone."

"I know," he said. "I am not doing it for you. I am doing it *because* of you. You have shown me what I am capable of, and I know that I can do more."

"What about your entailed estate?" she said. "I know you

have had it rebuilt, but do you think that we will ever live there?"

He was silent for a moment, and she knew that old memories were likely coming to the surface.

"What would you think about trying a holiday there and seeing how we liked it? Then we could decide."

"I think that is a wonderful idea."

The carriage pulled up in front of the Palace of Westminster, and Levi leaned over and kissed her on the forehead before holding her close.

"I love you."

"I love you too. Go show them who you are."

He nodded before emerging from the carriage, his shoulders tall and proud as he walked through the ornate, embellished entryway, and Siena's heart picked up speed. It was with reluctance that she asked the carriage to return her home, as it had been so long since she had been without Levi.

But at least it was only for a short time – even if the hours did seem to drag while he was away, as she wished for his return, to know what had occurred and how he had been received.

She had dinner with Eliza, sang Caroline to sleep, and lay in bed reading until he returned home, long into the night.

Siena heard the wheels of the carriage crunching the gravel outside, felt the house shift with the closing of the door, and anticipated her husband's footsteps as he came into the bedroom.

"Levi," she said as he backed into the room quietly, likely trying not to disturb her. "How was it?"

"I can hardly believe you are awake," he said, hurrying to her side. "It's late."

"I couldn't sleep, not knowing of your evening," she said, lifting her hands to his cheeks. "Well?"

He blinked, disbelief covering his face for a moment. "They clapped. Standing."

"What do you mean?" she asked, confused.

"When I entered," he explained. "They stood and clapped for me. Apparently, they found my war efforts heroic, and with McGregor's trial and punishment, they know I didn't kill my brother. So... they clapped."

She searched his eyes, trying to determine his response.

"What did you think of that?"

He took her hands within his, kneading them gently as he thought about it.

"I was honored, in part, I cannot lie," he said. "Although I was also reminded that they only feel this way now that my name has been cleared. But I am accepted, no matter my visage, so I will welcome their recognition. It is the only way to move on."

"We have a good life, do we not?" she asked softly.

"We do," he said. "No more running."

"No more running," she agreed, and they sealed their vow with a kiss.

THE END

* * *

Dear reader,

I hope you enjoyed Siena and Levi's story! I would love to know what you thought of them all! You are always welcome to email me at ellie@elliestclair.com, post in my facebook group or, of course, leave a review.

Did you enjoy Eliza and Fitz? I hope so, because their story is coming soon! Keep reading for a preview on the next pages, or head to Amazon to download the story here.

In the meantime, if you love some mystery sprinkled in

with your romance and haven't yet read my Remingtons of the Regency series, then be sure to start with The Mystery of the Debonair Duke!

If you haven't yet signed up for my newsletter, I would love to have you join us! You will receive Unmasking a Duke for free, as well as links to giveaways, sales, new releases, and stories about my coffee addiction, my struggle to keep my plants alive, and how much trouble one loveable wolf-lookalike dog can get into.

<u>www.elliestclair.com/ellies-newsletter</u>

Or you can join my Facebook group, Ellie St. Clair's Ever Afters, and stay in touch daily.

Until next time, happy reading!

WITH LOVE,

Ellie

Her Daring Earl
Noble Pursuits Book 2

HOW DOES a man fix his reputation, become respected in Parliament, and find husbands for his seven sisters?

By marrying a demure, respectable young woman of course. Fate, however, has other plans when Lord Fitzroy must hurriedly leave London after multiple attempts on his life.

He certainly never planned on Lady Eliza. In fact, he had deliberately avoided her in the past for she — far from demure or respectable — proved far too tempting.

When she makes him an intriguing offer, he cannot stop himself from giving in. She surprises him in more ways than one, and soon he's not sure if he should be more scared of her or whoever is trying to take his life.

HER DARING EARL - CHAPTER ONE

It was an impossible task.

Marrying off all seven of his sisters?

Sisters who, while all intriguing in their own way, were not exactly what most men of the *ton* would consider marriage material?

It would take a miracle.

Fitz watched them as they practically pranced around the ballroom. Well, five of them. Two of them were not yet old enough to attend such events.

Thank goodness.

He could barely handle the first five.

"Having a good time?"

Fitz turned at the voice, his smile breaking free when he recognized his long-time friend, Baxter Munroe. The man who had very few flaws, but for one inescapable one – his sister. Some would say it was the mustache that adorned his face, but Fitz appreciated the way it flourished and how the man wore it without shame.

"I will have a much better time once my mother takes my sisters home," Fitz said, running a hand through his hair, unable to help the laugh that escaped. The duty of his sisters should cause him a great deal of consternation, but he couldn't allow his thoughts about it to deepen too extensively or he would never be able to focus on anything else.

"They're a lively lot," Baxter said, taking a sip of his drink as he watched the girls. They should be standing demurely on the side of the dance floor, waiting to be asked for a dance or a turn about the room. But no. Not Fitz's sisters. Instead, they were moving back in forth in time to the music, dancing with one another, unable to quietly wait – except for Sloane, who looked about ready to fall asleep.

"They're not unlike you," Baxter commented, eyeing Fitz from the corner of his eyes.

"What's that supposed to mean?" Fitz asked, although he was already chuckling, knowing exactly what it meant. He was also not one to wait around idly.

Baxter only shook his head. "Thank goodness I've only one sister to marry off – and my father is still around to worry about her."

That shortened Fitz's laugh. He didn't want to think about Baxter's sister. She caused him more consternation than his own.

"Why is your mother in such a hurry suddenly?" Baxter asked. "What has changed?"

"Dot is four and twenty. Far older than young women should be to be married, at least according to my mother. All Dot wants to do, unfortunately, is become a midwife. A midwife! Can you believe such a thing? My mother is beside herself and refuses to allow her to take on such common work. Of course, Dot has a mind of her own and you can hardly barricade a woman her age in her bedchamber, so my mother has tasked me with finding someone for her – and the others, at least the ones that are old enough."

"You have quite the job ahead of you."

"Don't I know it. I've practically begged half of the men here to dance with them, but I've heard every excuse there is as to why they cannot. Lost all humility I ever had to begin with."

Baxter laughed long and loud at that as Fitz finally sighed, shaking his head. "My parents really should have ensured they attended all of their dance lessons instead of the other pursuits they busied themselves with. Now they cannot find a dance partner due to all of these men who fear having their toes stepped on."

"Well, luckily for you, Fitz, I am a brave man."

Fitz looked up at Baxter with more hope than he should have dared felt. "You'll dance with them?"

"One of them," Baxter said with a slight look of horror flashing over his face. "Do not get too excited."

"One is wonderful," Fitz said, taking Baxter's drink out of his hand and setting it down before he could change his mind, leading him over to where his sisters waited. "Start with Dot."

"Start? I just said—"

"Here we are. Dot, Lord Anderson here has a question for you."

Baxter shot him a quick look that was part disdain, part amusement before reaching out and taking Dot's hand, bowing low over it.

"Lady Dot, would you permit me a dance?"

Dot, with her usual no-nonsense expression affixed to her face which Fitz knew was very similar to his features, looked at first Baxter and then Fitz with skepticism before nodding her head. "Very well. It will appease Mother."

Baxter appeared flummoxed, unable to articulate a response as he led her out onto the dance floor, where couples were gathering for the next set. He leaned in as he passed Fitz. "Favor for a favor, Fitz. Find my sister."

Fitz closed his eyes for a moment, wondering if he could pretend that he didn't hear Baxter's request. But the man had a point. If he didn't return the favor, how could he ever ask the man for anything again?

He reluctantly turned around to look for her.

Only to find her standing right behind him, her arms crossed and a jaunty smile on her face as though she was expecting him, and knew exactly what he was thinking.

A terrifying thought, indeed.

* * *

"Lady Eliza." Fitz took a visible intake of breath before forcing a smile.

Of all the men in all of London, it had to be him. Here. Now. If she'd had time once she realized it was him standing in front of her, she would have backed away before he had noticed her. She had allowed her intrigue in the interaction between her brother and Dot to distract her. "Lovely to see you."

"Oh, Fitz," she rolled her eyes. "Don't do that. Not to me."

"I am sure that I do not know what you are talking about," he said smartly, rocking back and forth on his heels.

"Drop the act, Fitz."

He eyed her for a moment before his lips curled up into his signature smile and his heels dropped onto the ground. "Very well. Lady Eliza, it has not been long enough since we last saw one another. I am sorry that we are meeting again."

"There, was that so hard?" She practically beamed, even though her feet were telling her to run as fast as she could away from this man. Other parts of her were saying something else, which was precisely the problem, and why she had no business being anywhere near him.

"Eliza!" Henrietta gasped from beside her, but Hen didn't

understand. She never had. She loved her brother, and rightly so. Eliza was sure he was a wonderful brother to his seven sisters, two of which – twins, Henrietta and Sloane – were close friends of hers. But he wasn't Eliza's brother. Not by a long shot. And he wasn't so wonderful to her.

"Would you like to dance?" he asked, the question clearly painful for him to ask.

"No," she answered honestly. "But if I deny you with my mother and the rest of the *ton* looking on, then there is sure to be, at the very least, scandal, and far more likely and annoying, my mother will pester me to know why I would turn down a man who is such close friends with our family and who has been so supportive of us. I do hate to disappoint my mother after all she has done for me."

"You are such a wonderful daughter."

"Do not patronize me."

"Very well," he said, lifting his brows. "But you do realize that you could have been like every other woman who is asked to dance by a man she despises and simply said yes."

"Where is the fun in that? Besides, I'm not doing this for you. I'm doing it for my brother. He needs to make it look as though he is doing his duty in trying to marry me off and he thinks by asking you to return his favor and dance with me, it will be good enough."

"Must you be so forthright?"

"I must."

"What has gotten into you two?" Henrietta asked, looking between Eliza and her brother. "Dance or not but please do not subject me to such tension."

"Very well. My apologies, Hen," Eliza said as she reached out and practically snatched Fitz's arm. He said nothing as he led her to the middle of the floor where the musicians had just struck up a waltz. Of course. It had to be a waltz. One of his arms came around her, the other took her hand in his.

"It's been a while since we danced," he murmured against her ear, his breath hot on her neck. Eliza hated herself for the involuntary shiver he evoked within her.

"Not long enough," she countered as stoutly as she could, becoming even more annoyed when he ignored her.

"I do not believe I have seen you since we were both at Greystone with Siena and Levi. What a time that was."

"It most certainly was," she said, wondering if it was the first time they had agreed on something.

"I hope you noticed how well-behaved I was during our time there."

"What does it matter what I think?" She said, furrowing her brow and leaning back away from him so she could see into his face. "Besides, I am sure it must have been very difficult for you to go so long without a woman warming your bed."

A smirk began to play over his lips and Eliza knew him well enough to be aware that a joke had come to him, one that she would likely rather not hear.

"It must have been difficult for you to resist volunteering for the job."

"I would rather sleep in the barn."

Then he did something that surprised her more than she would like.

He threw back his head and laughed out loud.

His laugh was one of those that was so overwhelmingly contagious, loud and booming, that all of the couples nearby and even those close to the other side of the dance floor turned toward them in both shock and interest to see what had so enraptured the earl.

Eliza lifted her hand off of his shoulder ever so slightly and smacked him. "Stop that."

"Why? You made the joke!"

"Everyone is staring."

"Do you care?" He asked, lifting a brow, and not for the first time, Eliza cursed him for how handsome he was.

"I do not. But my mother will. And your mother will. And then there will be hell to pay after this."

"I am a grown man, two and thirty. An earl. It doesn't matter what my mother thinks."

"Does it not?" Eliza said, lifting a brow and taking a small step backward. "Perhaps, then, we should go discuss with her your intentions on taking a bride. I am sure she has an opinion. In fact—"

"You will do no such thing," he practically growled, pulling her so quickly and tightly against his body that she gasped, feeling every hard muscle not otherwise cloaked in an abundance of fabric meld against her body. "My mother does not need to know of such things."

"Because you are scared of her," she teased.

"I am not."

"You are! Otherwise, you wouldn't pay her interest in marrying off your sisters any mind and you would let Dot do exactly what she wants to do.'

"And be a midwife?" He snorted. "I think not."

"She loves it."

"Just as I love new adventures but you are not going to find me traipsing around the countryside night and day to fulfill my dreams. I have a job to do, and I am not going to shirk it. Dot also needs to do what she must."

"Says who?"

"Says..." he blinked, and she knew she had him for a moment. He shook his head abruptly. "Society. My mother. My father."

"Your father is dead so he doesn't care. Your mother will be fine, and in fact, it seems to me she rather likes having her daughters nearby. She just thinks it is proper to marry them off. And you only care about society because of your political ambitions."

"I am an earl. I have my seat regardless of what people think of me."

She narrowed her eyes at him. "I know you. You want people to think that you have no cares in the world, but you want them to respect you so that they listen to what you say and put credit in your opinions."

He leaned in toward her, more eagerness in his stance than she had ever seen in him before. He was usually such a carefree, lackadaisical man. "I want to create change, Eliza. To do that, I need people to support me."

"What kind of change?" she asked, suddenly intrigued, even though the song was beginning to come to a close.

"What the hell?" he growled, causing Eliza to start.

"That is not exactly the language—"

But he had dropped his arms from her and left her, already walking away without another word.

"What in the world?" she muttered, knowing she should leave this be, but was unable to help her curiosity as she followed him across the dance floor in time to see him stop in front of Dot, whose hand was caught in that of a tall, thin man – Lord Mandrake, if she was not mistaken.

"Mandrake!" Fitz practically bellowed, causing Eliza to jump. He was not usually a man with a temper, at least as far as she knew – and she knew him better than she would like. "Get your hands off my sister!"

Her Daring Earl is available on Amazon and in Kindle Unlimited.

ALSO BY ELLIE ST. CLAIR

Noble Pursuits
Her Runaway Duke
Her Daring Earl

Reckless Rogues
The Duke's Treasure (prequel)
The Earls's Secret
The Viscount's Code
The Scholar's Key
The Lord's Compass
The Heir's Fortune

The Remingtons of the Regency
The Mystery of the Debonair Duke
The Secret of the Dashing Detective
The Clue of the Brilliant Bastard
The Quest of the Reclusive Rogue

The Unconventional Ladies
Lady of Mystery
Lady of Fortune
Lady of Providence
Lady of Charade

The Unconventional Ladies Box Set

To the Time of the Highlanders

A Time to Wed

A Time to Love

A Time to Dream

Thieves of Desire

The Art of Stealing a Duke's Heart

A Jewel for the Taking

A Prize Worth Fighting For

Gambling for the Lost Lord's Love

Romance of a Robbery

Thieves of Desire Box Set

The Bluestocking Scandals

[Designs on a Duke](#)

[Inventing the Viscount](#)

[Discovering the Baron](#)

[The Valet Experiment](#)

[Writing the Rake](#)

[Risking the Detective](#)

[A Noble Excavation](#)

[A Gentleman of Mystery](#)

The Bluestocking Scandals Box Set: Books 1-4

The Bluestocking Scandals Box Set: Books 5-8

Blooming Brides

A Duke for Daisy

A Marquess for Marigold

An Earl for Iris

A Viscount for Violet

The Blooming Brides Box Set: Books 1-4

Happily Ever After
The Duke She Wished For
Someday Her Duke Will Come
Once Upon a Duke's Dream
He's a Duke, But I Love Him
Loved by the Viscount
Because the Earl Loved Me

Happily Ever After Box Set Books 1-3
Happily Ever After Box Set Books 4-6

The Victorian Highlanders
Duncan's Christmas - (prequel)
[Callum's Vow](#)
[Finlay's Duty](#)
[Adam's Call](#)
[Roderick's Purpose](#)
[Peggy's Love](#)

[The Victorian Highlanders Box Set Books 1-5](#)

Searching Hearts
Duke of Christmas (prequel)
Quest of Honor
Clue of Affection
Hearts of Trust
Hope of Romance
Promise of Redemption

Searching Hearts Box Set (Books 1-5)

Christmas

Christmastide with His Countess

Her Christmas Wish

Merry Misrule

A Match Made at Christmas

A Match Made in Winter

Standalones

Always Your Love

The Stormswept Stowaway

A Touch of Temptation

Regency Summer Nights Box Set

Regency Romance Series Starter Box Set

For a full list of all of Ellie's books, please see www.elliestclair.com/books.

ABOUT THE AUTHOR

Ellie has always loved reading, writing, and history. For many years she has written short stories, non-fiction, and has worked on her true love and passion -- romance novels.

In every era there is the chance for romance, and Ellie enjoys exploring many different time periods, cultures, and geographic locations. No matter when or where, love can always prevail. She has a particular soft spot for the bad boys of history, and loves a strong heroine in her stories.

Ellie and her husband love nothing more than spending time at home with their children and Husky cross. Ellie can typically be found at the lake in the summer, pushing the stroller all year round, and, of course, with her computer in her lap or a book in hand.

She also loves corresponding with readers, so be sure to contact her!

www.elliestclair.com
ellie@elliestclair.com

- facebook.com/elliestclairauthor
- x.com/ellie_stclair
- instagram.com/elliestclairauthor
- amazon.com/author/elliestclair
- goodreads.com/elliestclair
- bookbub.com/authors/elliest.clair
- pinterest.com/elliestclair

Printed in Great Britain
by Amazon